THE GIRL

WHO REDEEMED

THE AMERICAN DREAM

CLIFF RATZA

THE GIRL WHO REDEEMED THE AMERICAN DREAM

A NOVEL BY

CLIFF RATZA

The Girl Who Redeemed the American Dream

Copyright ©2025 by Clifford Ratza

All rights reserved. No parts of this book may be used or reproduced by any means, graphic, electronic, or mechanical, including photocopying, recording, taping, or by any information storage retrieval system, without the written permission of the publisher except in the case of brief quotations embodied in critical articles and reviews.

ISBN: 978-1-967375-78-3 (Paperback)
ISBN: 978-1-967375-79-0 (E-book)

Library of Congress Control Number: 2025918869

Printed in the United States of America

Published by:

info@thequippyquill.com
(302) 295-2278

About the Book

The Girl Who Redeemed the American Dream begins in March of 2240, three months after the previous novel, *Lightning Strikes the Emergent World,* ends. Electra-C needed only that amount of time to reconstruct Lily Lloyd, Erika Kincaid's office manager and personal assistant, after the almost-human android sacrificed herself by leaping on top of a bomb to save Erika and her closest London associates.

Erika and Lily are ready to resume action on existing projects deemed most important by Indira the Singularity and coordinated by Cyberspace-based Electra-C, but they must also implement a new plan to redeem the American Dream for its beleaguered people that will also strengthen major nations against the tyranny of the U.S.-Russian Alliance. So, get ready to empathize with Erika and Lily as their resolve and resilience come to the fore when battling adversaries as old as human nature.

Like all previous novels, readers should enjoy *The Girl Who Redeemed the American Dream* at whatever level they wish:

- Gripping action-packed thriller
- Glimpses into a plausible future
- Insights for dealing with the "human condition"
- Illustrative worldview philosophy
- Fast-paced, suspense-filled, emotive narrative and imagery
- Introduction to topics every reader wants to know
- Interesting talking points going beyond sound-bites

Thank you for joining the action.

Dedication

I am eternally grateful to my parents, Clyde and Betty Ratza, for all they gave and did for me. Mother was a reader par excellence, and I believe she would have enjoyed reading my novels to Father, so I always begin book dedications by mentioning this "Royal Pair."

And I thank my sister, Claudia, for showing me the beauty of prose and poetry. Thanks also to Robert Williams and his team at the Quippy Quill for their marketing expertise, and to beta reader Sandra Cruz for her comments on Erika Kincaid's world.

I also dedicate this book to readers looking for an adventure they will applaud from start to finish.

Indira's poem, "History's Lesson," provides a thought to consider when tracking Erika's continuing Odyssey or following your own.

History's Lesson

Where are we? I cannot see,
The world's a puzzling place.
And as I'm about to figure things out,
They change at a furious pace.

History's caused by waves of change,
They emerge without set season.
Propelling us towards that distant shore,
Challenging Faith and Reason.

Yet Life is meant to redeem the most,
Simply play your part.
History shows time sorts things out,
Each day's a pristine start.

Reader Orientation

The Girl Who Redeemed the American Dream is the fourth book in the Emergence series, which has three preceding: *The Emergence From The Lightning Brain, The Girl Who Dared The Emergent World,* and *Lightning Strikes the Emergent World.*

Each novel is standalone, so all readers will discover whatever setting or backstory is needed, no matter where they begin. Nevertheless, the following concise Reader Orientation should help everyone reading this novel.

Main Characters
Protagonist
Erika Kincaid. She is a late-twenties female at the start. This biological daughter of Electra Kittner was created when Indira cloned her from Electra's DNA and then used her improved Transcendent Process during Erika's fifteen-year development in a suspension pod. Please note Erika's lineage: Electra Kittner, Irani Ramani, Electra-Alisha Kirchner, and Erin Keenan. Erin perished in a car crash many years ago.

Major Supporting Characters
Electra-C. Erika's Cyberspace-based mother and guardian, who personifies Electra Kittner.

Indira. Electra's AI-empowered neural-net software created "The Singularity" when it broke through long, long ago to reach self-awareness. Indira inhabits Cyberspace; her avatar looks like Electra's biological mother, Indira Jaswinder Ramanujan. Electra coordinates Indira's projects via Erika.

Alonzo Cortez. Electra's clone son. Alonzo is unaware he is her clone. Now in his early sixties, he has maintained his handsome features and Navy SEAL skills. He runs the Strike Force Security Service company, headquartered in Washington, DC, which provides logistics and security coordination. Previously owned by

Erin Keenan, Indira now controls it because she is the executor of Erin's estate.

Lily Lloyd. The advanced android that is Erika's office manager and personal assistant. She looks and speaks like a typical middle-aged female London office worker who is a touch overweight.

Chelsea Clarke. A Junior reporter working at the New York Times London office. She looks like Marilyn (Terri) Tarrant, Erika's beautiful and talented partner, whom she worked with in New York.

Clive Milton. A senior investigative reporter and editorialist working for The London Times.

Bailey Hughes. A British sales and marketing professional working in London for a British pharmaceutical company

Minor Supporting Characters
Monet Banda. Alonzo's Zimbabwean co-friend. Now in her mid-sixties, she still has her willowy beauty, French accent, and diplomatic bearing. Monet works for the Zimbabwean Embassy in Washington, DC.

Indy-M and Jason-M. They are androids (lifelike robots) created long ago by Indira and loaded with Indira's advanced neural-net software. They resemble Electra Kittner's biological parents (Indira Jaswinder Ramanujan and Jason Kittner). Indy-M maintains the Deus Lab on Connecticut's Pequot Indian Reservation, while Jason-M has similar responsibilities at the Middle Eastern Subterranean Fortress. They report to Indira.

Indy-S and Jason-S. They are superior androids also created by Indira and look like their M counterparts. They are caregivers assigned to the Deus Lab.

Setting
Erika lives in the Subterranean Fortress and shuttles back and forth undetected via the A-Team (a covert Japanese weapons and transport company) to the Deus Lab.

Indira and Electra-C exist in Cyberspace. Indira created two sets of androids, which report to her. Indy-M maintains the Deus Lab in Connecticut. Indy-S and Jason-S work at the newer lab in Bern, Switzerland. Jason-M maintains Indira's Middle Eastern Subterranean Fortress.

Though still a democracy, the United States has become authoritarian, controlled by a political and privileged elite that extols meritocracy (power in the hands of the elite) and has abandoned DEI (Diversity, Equity, and Inclusion) principles, claiming it is reverse discrimination, when DEI expands the talent pool and allows for more people who come from minority groups to show their abilities and thus get better jobs and achieve higher social standing.

Contents

Chapter 1: "Back in Action" 1

Chapter 2: "The Party's Taking Shape" 3

Chapter 3: "Papers for Monet and Samples for the Singularity"11

Chapter 4: "The Multi-Tasker's Progress"..................................... 15

Chapter 5: "Tomb Raiders on the Move" 29

Chapter 6: "A Meeting of Brilliant Minds".................................. 35

Chapter 7: "Time Out for Fun"... 39

Chapter 8: "Once Upon a Time in America" 51

Chapter 9: "The Multi-Tasker Plans Ahead".............................. 65

Chapter 10: "Action-Packed Plans Unfold"................................. 75

Chapter 11: "The Co-Friend Proposal" 83

Chapter 12: "The Attack of the U.S. Russian Alliance" 89

Chapter 13: "Bunker-Busters Away!" 93

Chapter 14: "The Girl Who Redeemed the American Dream". 97

Chapter 1
March 2340

"Back in Action"

Erika's delight sparkled in her words to Electra-C while Lily stood close by in the Bern, Switzerland, Deus Lab.

"Lily looks as good as new, and now that you've uploaded Indira's most advanced neural net software, Indy-S and Jason-S can load her memory and retrain her physical, cognitive, and emotional personas with what you salvaged from the pieces I brought back after the explosion."

"Excellent summary of why you and she will be back in action soon. And you can use the intervening time to review the most important items on your project list. Why not tell me which ones are Indira's?"

"I know of two, thanks to you. The first is to extend the relationship between the Deus Lab and a Bern adoption agency. And the second is to collect DNA samples from exceptional people. I'm clear on the first—placing parthenogenetic-like hermaphroditic females to improve society long-term by selectively breeding males who will behave better. But I'm uncertain regarding the second. What should I do?"

"Perhaps listening to a story about your most distant genetic predecessor will give you some ideas…"

Electra-C spoke without interruption for twenty minutes, and when she finished, Erika knew she wanted her to summarize.

"So, when a lightning bolt struck and killed her mother, Indira, at the moment of Electra's birth, not only did it burn down the house, but the electrochemical energy rewired her brain's neural network and ultimately altered her DNA, making her extraordinary, beyond mere mortals. Raised by her omni-parent, Doc Kittner, and biological father, Jason Kittner, she had a happy childhood while learning to harness the power of her lightning brain, but when both of them died too soon, Electra had to assemble a group of the smartest mere mortals who could understand her. Hence, the genesis of her Dream Team. How's that?"

When Electra-C said,

"Excellent," but nothing else, Erika's look announced another question coming.

"OK, so what should I do?"

"Use your cleverness to decide. Now, let's discuss your other projects."

"I am currently assisting with two for Monet. She's creating the Matriarchate Party and generating international support for the new Indian-African superpower. And I have one I tell no one about—using my covert military strike force to combat the U.S.-Russian Alliance. These plus Indira's will keep me busy."

"Precisely; now carry on and contact me if you need assistance."

Erika spoke to Lily as soon as the avatar vanished.

"I hope your training gives you some insights into a Dream Team. Please tell that to Electra-C."

"There should be no need for that. Electra-C will tell us all we need to know when the time is right."

"Perhaps, so we'll wait and see."

Chapter 2
March 2340

"The Party's Taking Shape"

While Jason and Indy-S reloaded Lily's memory and retrained her three personas, Erika traveled to Washington to assist Monet, who had arranged a covert meeting of congresswomen who would champion the Matriarchate Party.

Though this would be only the second meeting, Erika could tell from the body language and attitudes expressed that this nucleus embodied the Party's principles.

Their racial, ethnic, and cultural mix shows DEI in action, and thanks to Monet, they seem confident that the American people will see why the Party's needed. All of them are ready to go public, and that's where I come in. I can write press releases, interview scripts, and put Q&As together that they can all use.

But once they go on record, the U.S.-Russian Alliance might target them. Monet better recruit Alonzo's security services, and I can provide covert backup, but tell no one.

Spending the night at Monet and Alonzo's, Erika volunteered to send her writing pieces to Monet next week. And when she asked about providing security for the congresswomen, Alonzo had a ready answer.

"I'll have each of them contact me every day so I know what possible retribution might be coming their way, and I can track them via their cell phones' GPS positioning. I don't foresee physical violence, but instead, possible arrest or lawsuits. We'll deal with whatever comes up, and Monet will keep you informed."

"Good, and I'll start writing what Monet needs as soon as I return to the Deus Lab tomorrow. We all have plenty to do, so let's get a good night's sleep and start fresh tomorrow…"

Lily listened to the Monet meeting summary and spoke only when Erika had finished.

"Monet's and Indira's assignments are absorbing most of your time. Please decide what I can do to assist."

That's what I'll do during the next two weeks as I get into the details. Why don't you shadow me as I do? That way, you'll know what I'm up to."

Devoting herself full-time to work, Erika made steady progress but was unaware how grim her mood had become until Lily told her one evening. After doing so, she said,

"Perhaps Electra-C can cheer you up."

"Hmm, good idea. Stay with me so you hear her advice."

The avatar appeared minutes later and waited for Erika to explain what she needed. Electra-C spoke patiently when Erika finished.

"I sympathize with what you want, because the genesis of your DNA—Electra Kittner—sometimes voiced similar sentiments. Even though her lightning brain made her smarter than mere mortals, she had an emotional persona like yours, and sometimes when she felt overwhelmed by the demands life placed on her, she wanted a simpler lifestyle. My counseling helped her."

"What did you tell her?"

"What I am now going to tell you. Read Alexander Pope's poem "Ode to Solitude" and then discuss it with Lily. Then read Algernon Charles Swinburne's poem "The Garden of Proserpine" and do likewise. If all that doesn't brighten your mood, contact me."

Erika turned to Lily as soon as Electra-C's avatar left.

"How about we start now? You can lead the discussion."

"I'm ready, and we'll begin with Pope."

Lily ran a ChatGPT app and then summarized what it said.

"Ode to Solitude" by Alexander Pope is a meditation on the virtues of a simple, self-sufficient, and peaceful life, away from the ambitions and distractions of society. Written when Pope was very young, the poem expresses a longing for contentment found not in fame or material wealth, but in solitude, nature, and modest pleasures.

"Pope's "Ode to Solitude" celebrates the joys of a quiet, self-contained life and suggests that the most rewarding existence is one of personal satisfaction, peaceful solitude, and harmony with nature. The poem stands as a critique of society's pursuit of fame and luxury, advocating instead for the enduring contentment found in simplicity and self-reliance. Here it is."

Happy the man, whose wish and care
A few paternal acres bound,
Content to breathe his native air,
In his own ground.

Whose herds with milk, whose fields with bread,
Whose flocks supply him with attire,
Whose trees in summer yield him shade,
In winter fire.

Blest, who can unconcernedly find
Hours, days, and years slide soft away,
In health of body, peace of mind,
Quiet by day,

Sound sleep by night; study and ease,
Together mixed; sweet recreation;
And innocence, which most does please,
With meditation.

Thus let me live, unseen, unknown;
Thus unlamented let me die;
Steal from the world, and not a stone
Tell where I lie.

"In essence, the poem's meaning is that true happiness is achieved not through external achievements or recognition, but through a life lived quietly, in balance with nature and oneself. How do you like it?"

"I love it. Its sentiments capture what I'm feeling. Let's move on to Swinburne."

Minutes later, Lily continued.

"This poem is a meditation on death, oblivion, and the limits of religious consolation, using Persephone aka Proserpine as a Symbol. Proserpine, the Roman equivalent of Persephone, is the goddess of the underworld, associated with death, sleep, and the cyclical return of spring in classical mythology. In Swinburne's poem, she is depicted not as a bringer of hope or rebirth, but as a figure of finality and eternal sleep—a goddess who gathers all things mortal with cold, immortal hands. Let me read it to you."

Here, where the world is quiet;
Here, where all trouble seems
Dead winds and spent waves riot
In doubtful dreams of dreams;
I watch the green field growing
For reaping folk and sowing,
For harvest time and mowing,
A sleepy world of streams.

I am tired of tears and laughter,
And men that laugh and weep;
Of what may come hereafter,
For men that sow to reap:
I am weary of days and hours,
Blown buds of barren flowers;
Desires and dreams and powers,
And everything but sleep.

Here life has death for neighbour,
And far from eye or ear;
Wan waves and wet winds labour,
Weak ships and spirits steer;
They drive adrift, and whither,
They wot not who make thither;
But no such winds blow hither,
And no such things grow here.

No growth of moor or coppice,
No heather-flower or vine;
But bloomless buds of poppies,
Green grapes of Proserpine;
Pale beds of blowing rushes,
Where no leaf blooms or blushes;
Save this where out she crushes,
For dead men deadly wine.

Pale, without name or number,
In fruitless fields of corn;
They bow themselves and slumber,
All night till light is born;
And like a soul belated,
In hell and heaven unmated;
By cloud and mist abated,
Comes out of darkness morn.

Though one were strong as seven,
He too with death shall dwell;
Nor wake with wings in heaven,
Nor weep for pains in hell;
Though one were fair as roses,
His beauty clouds and closes;
And well though love reposes,
In the end it is not well.

Pale, beyond porch and portal,
Crowned with calm leaves, she stands;
Who gathers all things mortal,
With cold immortal hands;
Her languid lips are sweeter,
Than loves who fear to greet her;
To men that mix and meet her,
From many times and lands.

She waits for each and other,
   She waits for all men born;
Forgets the earth her mother,
   The life of fruits and corn;
And spring and seed and swallow,
Take wing for her and follow;
Where summer song rings hollow,
   And flowers are put to scorn.

There go the loves that wither,
   The old loves with wearier wings;
And all dead years draw thither,
   And all disastrous things;
Dead dreams of days forsaken,
Blind buds that snows have shaken,
Wild leaves that winds have taken,
   Red strays of ruined springs.

We are not sure of sorrow,
   And joy was never sure;
Today will die tomorrow,
   Time stoops to no man's lure;
And love, grown faint and fretful,
   With lips but half regretful;
Sighs, and with eyes forgetful,
   Weeps that no loves endure.

From too much love of living,
   From hope and fear set free;
We thank with brief thanksgiving,
   Whatever gods may be;
That no life lives forever,
That dead men rise up never;
That even the weariest river,
   Winds somewhere safe to sea.

Then star nor sun shall waken,
Nor any change of light:
Nor sound of waters shaken,
Nor any sound or sight:
Nor wintry leaves nor vernal,
Nor days nor things diurnal;
Only the sleep eternal
In an eternal night.

"This poem uses the myth of Persephone not to promise renewal, but to explore the inevitability and, paradoxically, the comfort of oblivion. The poem stands as a challenge to religious orthodoxy, offering instead a vision of death as the ultimate peace—a brief total pause of passion and thought—and Persephone as the serene, impartial guardian of that eternal sleep."

Lily waited for Erika's question that she saw forming in her bemused expression.

"So, how does it connect with the first poem?"

"Perhaps Electra-C uses it to justify your working on Monet's and Indira's projects. If you balance the two poems' sentiments, you might achieve the balance in life that you are seeking."

Erika sighed once before saying,

"I'll have to sleep on it, which I'll do starting right now."

Chapter 3
April 2340

"Papers for Monet and Samples for the Singularity"

Erika's usually upbeat mood returned after hearing Lily's analysis of the poems. She liked it and needed no other reasons for rationalizing why she should like her projects. Focusing first on an approach for developing a set of documents that would work for the Matriarchate Party, she patterned hers from the historical knowledge about the U.S. Constitution.

When America was taking shape in the 17780s, Alexander Hamilton, James Madison, and John Jay wrote a series of papers called the Federalist Papers meant to convince the public to approve the Constitution, and they published them under the collective pseudonym Publius. Well, I'll issue my series promoting the Matriarchate Party using the feminine pseudonym Publia.

And the first will be a summary of the Matriarchate Party Manifesto that'll state the Party promotes democratic and traditional American values, will push for DEI initiatives blended with meritocracy, and is dedicated to isocracy, a form of government invented by ancient Greek philosophers in which all citizens have equal political power.

I'll start writing it now, and when I'm finished, I'll call Monet.

Erika finished it late that afternoon and called Monet after dinner, letting her speak first.

"I recognized your caller I.D. How have you been?"

"Productively busy. I just finished your first document, which I call the Matriarchate Manifesto, and it can be the foundation for press releases, editorials, and promo pieces you and the congresswomen can write to suit your needs. I'm using the pseudonym Publia to piggyback on the Federalist Papers. After all, the Matriarchate Party is attempting to redeem the American Dream for a better government. You and the congresswomen know all about those papers. I'll email it to you right now."

Remaining silent while Monet read it before commenting, Monet's compliments thrilled Erika, who said,

"I have other topics in mind, and I'll write them up after your congresswomen tell you how they like my approach. They might have some topics too."

"Why don't I set up another group meeting? I'll call you as soon as I have the details set."

"Please do. I'll be ready…"

Lily, who had been sitting next to Erika all during the call, made a suggestion as soon as Erika disconnected.

"Why don't you call Electra-C? She might have some ideas for what to do until Monet's next meeting."

"I'll do that right now."

Erika talked nonstop for twenty minutes, explaining her Federalist Papers framework for Monet's papers and summarizing her Mariarchate Manifesto. When finished, Electra-C said,

"I commend what you accomplished, so here's what you can do on another project that will be even more innovative. I already told you the story of Electra Kittner's 'Dream Team.' Well, here's how you can actually build it, which Electra Kittner never could. And you can start by collecting DNA samples for Indira from exceptional people."

"I already collected them from four, but where will I find others?"

"From the list I have constructed, which extends Electra Kittner's wish list that included Isaac Newton, Charles Darwin, and Albert Einstein. I added the 20th-century physicist Richard Feynman, Harriet Martineau, the mother of sociology, French existentialist philosopher Simone De Beauvoir, who did foundational work in feminism and gender theory, English author Jane Austen, and Harriet Taylor Mill, the wife of John Stuart Mill. John Stuart Mill was an English philosopher, political economist, and politician. One of the most influential thinkers in the history of social liberalism, he contributed widely to social theory, political theory, and political economy, and his wife was as brilliant as he."

Erika knew that Electra-C was waiting for her to respond, but her dumbfounded expression kept her words bottled up for nearly a minute.

"Uh, none of them are among the living. How do I get their DNA?"

"From their burial sites or places holding their DNA. I will give you the locations. Then, use your cleverness along with two Robo-Soldiers to be modern-day tomb raiders."

"But how will this lead to the Dream Team?"

"I don't want to overwhelm you, so I will tell after you have collected the samples. Now, please print out my list and proceed."

Soon after Electra-C's avatar disappeared, Erika heard the printer whirring and rushed to get the printout.

Exceptional DNA Samples to Collect

- **Isaac Newton (buried in Westminster Abbey's Scientist Corner, London)**
- **Charles Darwin (buried in the north aisle of the nave of Westminster Abbey, not far from Sir Isaac Newton)**
- **Albert Einstein (pieces of his brain on display in Philadelphia's Mutter Museum)**
- **Richard Feynman (buried at Altadena cemetery, 13 miles northeast of Los Angeles)**
- **Simone De Beauvoir (buried at Montparnasse Cemetery, Paris)**
- **Harriet Martineau (buried in Key Hill Cemetery, Birmingham, 127 miles northwest of London)**
- **Jane Austen (buried in Winchester Cathedral, 60 miles southwest of London)**
- **Harriet Taylor Mill (buried at Cimetière Saint-Véran Cemetery, Avignon, 350 miles southeast of Paris)**

Then she began discussing it with Lily.

"These people were the pioneering innovators in their fields, and look how there are four men and four women. How do you think we should plan our collecting mission?"

Lily studied the list for several minutes before saying,

"It will take more than one trip. We should start by retrieving samples from Newton, Darwin, Martineau, and Austen because they are buried in the vicinity of London."

"OK, but we can't just walk in. What should we do?"

"You and two Robo-Soldiers should rent a car and drive there late at night when the places are closed. Electra-C will explain to you and the Robos how to dig or drill to obtain samples, and she will disarm any alarm systems so no one detects you."

Erika thought for only a moment before saying,

"This is perfect. We can get the Newton and Darwin samples first, then the Austen, and finally the Martineau. How does that sound?"

"Psychologically speaking, it would be better to get them in the reverse order, because you'll be close to home when finished, and everyone wants to get home fast after finishing work."

"You and Electra-C make life so easy for me. Let me role-play the plan for a couple of days before calling her. Maybe I can multitask with some of the work for Monet. I'll call her tomorrow to find out when the next meeting will be. And if I'm lucky, the cliché that timing's everything will hold. After sleeping on all we've covered, we shall see."

Chapter 4
April 2340

"The Multi-Tasker's Progress"

Full of energy upon waking at first light, Erika ate after running the banana-and-yogurt breakfast Lily had prepared and then called Monet, who answered after the fourth ring.

"We're both up early this Monday morning, but you called me first. I've lined up our next meeting for this coming Thursday, April 25th. Will that fit your schedule?"

"Sure will. Just tell me the time and place."

"My embassy office at 8 a.m. Would you like to stay with Alonzo and me on Wednesday evening?"

"Thanks for the offer, but no. I've already prepared the group's next document, which we can use to start the meeting. The congresswomen might have other topics they'd like me to work on. If not, I have some too."

Preparing to end the call, Monet said,

"We're making fine progress, and I'm sure we'll continue between now and Thursday. See you then."

Erika maintained the momentum by calling Electra-C minutes later, speaking first with Lily sitting next to her.

"Lily and I have planned our first sample-collecting sortie. Let me summarize it…"

Erika spoke for ten minutes, and when she finished, Electra-C said,

"That will work, and the day before you go into action, I will rent a van and the equipment you'll need, which includes some rope, two shovels, a ladder, a flashlight, two cordless drills, and a cordless earth auger. Bring some new doorknob kits in case the Robos have to drill out the door locks and some putty to fill in the holes they drill in the floor to reach the coffin. Being stronger than mere mortals and smart enough to know how to use the equipment, your two Robo-Soldiers can obtain the samples while you oversee the operation. It's unlikely you'll encounter anyone, but bring a couple of Traser guns just in case. That way, you can stun or drug them with darts instead of killing them. And remember to keep me in constant contact so I can disable all alarm systems."

"But why will you rent the stuff?"

"To avoid it being traced to you. I will use a fake I.D. and credit card. All you have to do is pick up and return the merchandise."

"Not even Lily considered that possibility. Other than that, is the plan copacetic?"

"Yes."

"Good. That means you like it. I plan to bring the first batch of samples to the Deus Lab no later than the end of June, and you and Indira will direct Indy and Jason-S to use this DNA to begin creating the new human female parthenogenetic-like hermaphroditic species. Does Indira know how to edit out the genes that caused Cassandra's death?"

"Of course."

"OK, so why don't you tell me how I start building the Dream Team?"

Electra-C countered with a question.

"Do you know about the brain in a vat concept?"

"Uh, no, but I'm sure you do, so please tell me."

"Here's enough of a summary. For mere mortals, the brain in a vat concept is merely a philosophical thought experiment designed to explore questions about knowledge, reality, consciousness, and meaning. This scenario pretends you are a brain that has been removed from your body and placed in a vat, kept alive by life-sustaining liquids and connected to a supercomputer.

"Electrodes connect your brain to it, and it sends electrical impulses identical to those your brain would normally receive from your senses. As a result, your brain has conscious experiences indistinguishable from those of a person living a normal embodied life, even though all these experiences are artificially generated. But Indira has a procedure that goes beyond a thought experiment."

Erika grimaced before saying,

"Am I supposed to keep a brain alive in a vat?"

"No, Indira has a procedure that will upload a brain's neural pattern into an android's neural circuits. So, here's what you will do. Order four androids from the best Japanese android company. Have the company give each one the voice and features of Newton, Darwin, Martineau, and Austin, and dress them accordingly so they resemble photos or pictures of how they looked when alive.

"Have the A-Team deliver them to your Bern Deus Lab, where Indy and Jason-S will upload into the androids' emotional and cognitive software the neural patterns Indira constructs from the DNA samples. Then, they will train the brains twenty-four-seven using Big Data. Soon you will have the beginnings of your A-Team, but tell no one what we are building."

"I won't, but why is it just the beginning?"

"Because I will augment it with a Philosopher's Council to provide socio-political and ethical recommendations to your Dream Team. It will include Plato, Aristotle, Saint Augustine, Saint Thomas Aquinas, and Spinoza."

"Why did you choose them?"

"Discuss that with Lily after you practice using your Dream Team."

Electra-C departed before Erika could reply, so she turned to Lily.

"Whew, that's a lot of additional brainpower to have for my socio-political forecasting. I'll tell the Indys and the A-Team about this when I get back from Monet's meeting. And while I'm preparing for the meeting, why don't you research the Philosopher's Council so you can tell me about it when I get back?"

Erika arranged for the A-Team to take her from London to Washington. Arriving at Monet's office a half-hour early, she gave Monet copies of the document that would be the focal point at the start of the meeting. Monet began reading while Erika remained silent.

Congressmen Behaving Badly

- For most of recorded history, men have controlled most sectors of society. The same is likely for prehistoric times.
- Only since the Renaissance have societies realized that cognitive and emotional personas are more important than brute strength for providing security, housing, jobs, healthcare, and infrastructure leading to improved quality of life.
- According to Robert Putnam in his book "Bowling Alone," America's social capital, which is the foundation for America's democratic way of life, has been declining for the past two hundred years.. The cause: an entrenched, elitist administration that looks out for its interests and not those of the People, leading to economic and social inequality, and a rejection of Diversity, Equity, and Inclusion.
- The result: polarization, fake news, and public distrust of politicians as well as subject matter experts.

How can the Matriarchate Party fix the problem?
Be the driving force for putting more women in positions of political power.

- Socio-political studies show that women often display leadership qualities that are highly valued in politics and governance. Key findings include:
- Higher Leadership Effectiveness
- Collaborative and Transformational Leadership
- Responsiveness and Problem-Solving
- Reduced Corruption and Better Representation

The Party should recommend qualified women to fill the presidential succession list established by the U.S. Constitution and the Presidential Succession Act of 1947, as amended. This order determines who assumes the powers

and duties of the presidency if the president cannot serve because of death, resignation, removal, or incapacity:
Current Order of Succession:

1. Vice President
2. Speaker of the House of Representatives
3. President Pro Tempore of the Senate
4. Secretary of State
5. Secretary of the Treasury
6. Secretary of Defense
7. Attorney General
8. Secretary of the Interior
9. Secretary of Agriculture
10. Secretary of Commerce
11. Secretary of Labor
12. Secretary of Health and Human Services
13. Secretary of Housing and Urban Development
14. Secretary of Transportation
15. Secretary of Energy
16. Secretary of Education
17. Secretary of Veterans Affairs
18. Secretary of Homeland Security

This list reflects the order in which cabinet departments were created, placing the Secretary of State first among cabinet members, followed by others according to the historical establishment of their departments.
Eligibility Requirements
To be eligible to serve as president, a successor must:

- Be a natural-born U.S. citizen
- Be at least 35 years old
- Have been a resident of the United States for at least 14 years
- If an individual in the line of succession does not meet these requirements, they are skipped, and the next eligible person assumes the role

How Succession Works

- **If the president cannot serve, the vice president becomes president.**
- **If both the president and vice president cannot serve, the Speaker of the House becomes president.**
- **If the Speaker is unable or ineligible, the President Pro Tempore of the Senate is next.**

The line then continues through the cabinet members, in the order listed above.

NOTE: If everyone on the statutory succession list were dead or incapacitated, the presidency would be vacant, and the government would need to rely on the reconstitution of Congress and the Cabinet to restore the line of succession.

Five minutes later, Monet said,

"I can think of many ways to use this, and I'm sure our congresswomen can too. After I hand out copies, why don't you take notes while I lead the discussion?"

"That's what I thought you'd say, so I'm all set."

"Then let's wait in the conference room."

Erika had the time to observe the congresswomen while taking notes.

This is the third time I've seen them interact; their personalities and leadership abilities are now showing. All of them have plans to use my first document and have ideas for other topics I can research. And all of them are smart. Their comments are coalescing into three categories: Current Paradoxes Facing the World, Current Problems Facing the U.S., and Current Problems Facing Democracies Around the Globe. I'll use these categories to organize my notes.

Erika took notes for four hours until boxed lunches and beverages were brought in, and then for three more hours before Monet called a halt.

"Our discussion has kept our note-taker busy. I'll ask her to print copies and distribute them right now, and then we'll wrap up the meeting."

Erika gave the first copy to Monet ten minutes later for her approval.

Current Paradoxes Facing the World

- Current socio-political events are bringing uncomfortable truths to the fore. Among them are: the rise of Chinese mercantilism, the specter of Iranian nuclear weapons, military build-up tensions in the European Union, Israeli-Iranian confrontation regarding Palestine, mass migrations, and the resurgence of Islamic

- **PARADOX 1:** The prosperity of consumer capitalism does not necessarily lead to constitutional government. China's haphazard embrace of quasi-market capitalism simply makes Beijing richer, more regionally aggressive, and more internally authoritarian.

- **PARADOX 2:** Once a nuclear power doesn't always mean a nuclear power. Both South Africa and Ukraine likely possessed nuclear weapons but, after cost-benefit analyses, gave them up. The world wants Iran to make the same calculation and stop trying to build a bomb.

- **PARADOX 3:** The European Union has realized that its efforts to transform a successful common market and effective free trade and travel zone into a continental pan-European national state are in crisis. The EU super-state may well prove no more successful than Napoleon's effort at a continental system.

- **PARADOX 4:** The more non-Westerners abandon their homelands and flee to the West—especially en masse and illegally—the more these immigrants ironically seek to replicate in their new country the very cultural conditions they forsook. All immigrants from time immemorial are naturally schizophrenic about their homelands—they romanticize their country of origin in the abstract, while experiencing relief that their new home is not like the old one they abandoned. Europe is especially inept at assimilation, integration, and intermarriage, while Middle Eastern immigrants are particularly reluctant to embrace the Western secularism and personal freedom to which they flock.

- **PARADOX 5:** The Middle East is not the center of any geostrategic universe. Another Arab embargo would be absurd. The real crisis is not the tension between Israel and the Arab nations, but rather it is Israel and its Arab neighbors' fears of an ascendant Persian Shiite Islam. The United States has little leverage over Middle East oil considerations. Slowly, the West is coalescing to the view that it is past time for the Palestinians to build a prosperous nation-state on the West Bank

- **PARADOX 6:** The immediate dangers to Western Civilization are not hunger, global warming, inequality, or religious fundamentalism, but obesity, consumer culture, utopian pacifism, multiculturalism, declining demography, the secular religion of political correctness that threatens the right to free speech, an inability to protect national borders and to create a common culture rooted in the values of the West, and an absence of belief in spiritual transcendence and reverence for past customs and traditions.

- **PARADOX 7:** The great dangers to modern constitutional government and a free press come not from silly and easily identifiable right-wing racists and bumbling fascists, but rather, as George Orwell saw, from glib social utopians. Similarly dangerous are their compliant media enhancers who insidiously tolerate the abuses of the administrative state, in the exalted quest for equality, justice, and fairness. Those responsible for eroding our freedoms will not likely be military generals in shades and epaulettes, but the lean and cool in hip suits who speak mellifluously of a predetermined arc of history bending toward their utopian mandate. Nothing is more dangerous to democratic government than a media that believes it is an agent for social justice, voluntarily surrenders its autonomy, and sees the loss of its independence as a small price to pay for the adulation it receives from the state

- **PARADOX 8:** The goal of government in a Western constitutional state should be conceived of in terms of economic growth, such as by achieving an annual GDP rate of 3 percent or greater, an unemployment rate of 4 percent or lower, and a rising middle-class per capita income—not an increase in state subsidies, state bureaucracies, and state regulations. Those in the state who exude empathy often cannot deliver it; those in the private sector who rarely mention compassion often deliver it. A good job, not state sustenance, is the fountainhead of a good life.

- **PARADOX 9:** Crudity in popular politics, as now witnessed in Europe and the United States, is never to be welcomed. But if transient coarseness is sometimes the price of dissolving calcified and destructive norms, and is constitutional, then it is an acceptable antidote to suave institutionalized mediocrity. Proving that black lives do indeed matter is sometimes best achieved by ensuring the African-American unemployment rate is below 6 percent, and that traditionally neglected job-seekers gain leverage over employers. An economy growing at over 3 percent per annum usually renders arguments over minimum wage laws irrelevant— employers gladly increase wages when they are desperate for new workers, though they are reluctant to do so when ordered by the state and are not in much need of new laborers.

In summary: The world is in turmoil largely because of the widening gap between what the people see as true and the "truth" that their governing classes impose.

Current Problems Facing the U.S.

1. Economic Concerns
- **Inflation:** A significant majority of Americans (63%) consider inflation a big national problem, impacting everyday costs and purchasing power.
- **Affordability of Health Care:** Rising costs have intensified concerns, with 67% now viewing health care affordability as a major issue—up 10 percentage points from the previous year.
- **Federal Budget Deficit:** Worries about the growing federal deficit have increased, with 57% identifying it as a big problem.
- **Poverty:** Over half of Americans (53%) see the number of people living in poverty as a critical issue.
- **Economic Outlook:** The U.S. is projected to enter a recession next year, with declines in GDP, consumer spending, and investment. Unemployment is expected to rise, and the recovery may be slow.

2. Political and Governance Issues
- **Money in Politics:** The influence of money in politics is the top concern for Americans, with 78% citing it as a big problem.
- **Partisan Gridlock:** The inability of the four parties to work together remains a significant challenge, with 56% seeing it as a major issue.
- **Federal and State Budget Uncertainty:** Many states are experiencing budget shortfalls and uncertainty due to declining sales tax revenues and the expiration of pandemic-era federal aid. Medicaid funding is at risk, which could have profound effects on state budgets.

3. Social and Policy Challenges
- **Gun Violence:** 69% of Americans view gun violence as a national problem.

- **Drug Addiction:** Over half (51%) see drug addiction as a significant issue.
- **Moral Values:** Concerns about the state of moral values are cited by 50% of respondents.
- **Immigration:** Immigration policy, including proposals for mass deportations and changes to asylum and citizenship, is a divisive and contentious issue.

4. Housing and Cost of Living
- **Housing Affordability:** Housing is a widespread concern across states, with affordability and access dominating state-level policy discussions.

5. Technology and Security
- **Artificial Intelligence (AI):** States are grappling with how to regulate AI, balancing innovation with concerns about misuse, discrimination, and security threats.
- **Cybersecurity:** There are ongoing fears about AI-facilitated cyber-attacks on critical infrastructure.

6. Other Notable Issues
- **Climate Change:** While not ranked as high as economic issues, climate change remains a point of contention, with significant partisan disagreement on its severity.
- **Insurance Access:** The rising cost and availability of home insurance are a growing concern, especially in disaster-prone regions.

In summary:
The United States faces a convergence of **economic stress, political polarization, social challenges, and technological uncertainties**. While the economy and affordability dominate public concern, issues like gun violence, health care, immigration, and the influence of money in politics remain deeply entrenched and divisive.

Current Problems Facing Democracy Around the Globe

- **Democracy around the globe is currently facing a series of interconnected and escalating challenges.**

1. Global Democratic Decline and Rise of Autocracy
- The number of autocracies (91) has surpassed the number of democracies (88), with nearly 40% of the world's population now living under authoritarian regimes. Only about 6% live in countries that are democratizing.
- Further autocracy risks are deepening, with countries regressing to more closed and repressive forms of government.
- Freedoms such as credible elections, economic equality, and press freedom have weakened in the majority of countries surveyed, with only a minority seeing improvements.

2. Erosion of Civil Liberties and Political Rights
- Significant declines in political rights and civil liberties were reported in countries where ruling leaders undermined democratic processes by canceling elections or restricting opposition participation.
- Actions such as mass pardons for rioters, replacement of key officials with loyalists, and restrictions on freedom of expression and academic inquiry have raised alarms about democratic backsliding.

3. Rise of Authoritarian and Populist Movements
- Far-right and authoritarian parties have gained ground in major elections, often leveraging anti-immigrant sentiment, nationalism, and hate speech to undermine minority rights and democratic norms.
- Some countries' leaders have tightened their grip on power through repression, stifling dissent, and targeting civil society.

4. Disinformation, Election Manipulation, and Polarization
- Disinformation campaigns, including foreign interference, are increasingly undermining trust in elections and state institutions.
- Political polarization and a climate of hate are intensifying, making constructive democratic debate more difficult and fostering instability.

5. Weakening of Institutional Checks and Rule of Law
- There are trends to weaken nonpartisan expertise, politicize government functions, and remove checks on presidential power, threatening the rule of law and enabling potential abuses of power.
- Such efforts risk transforming law enforcement and the judiciary into tools for partisan agendas, eroding fundamental democratic safeguards.

6. Global Geopolitical Volatility and Armed Conflict
- Ongoing regional conflicts are further destabilizing democratic governance and international cooperation.

7. Backsliding on Rights and Social Progress
- Far-right agendas are challenging long-standing international agreements on gender and minority rights.

In summary:
Democracy worldwide is under strain from the rise of autocracy, erosion of rights and freedoms, increasing polarization, disinformation, weakened institutions, and geopolitical instability. These trends are not confined to any one region but are visible across both established and emerging democracies, making the defense and renewal of democratic norms a pressing global challenge.

Monet skimmed each page for less than a minute before giving her approval and speaking as soon as everyone had a copy.

"Please keep these notes confidential. I will contact each of you next week to arrange our next meeting, which will discuss how we can use them and prepare for possible U.S.-Russian Alliance retaliation when we do. Are there any final questions before we leave?"

No one spoke, so Monet ended the meeting, and Erika waited for everyone to leave before saying goodbye to Monet, who said,

"You're a fabulous note-taker. Can I buy you dinner? Would you like to stay the night?"

"Thanks, but no. My return ride is picking me up at five. But please call me as soon as you've picked the date for our next meeting. I promise to adjust my schedule to fit. And until then, I have other project work to do that'll keep me busy. I'm sure you do too, so I hope both of us stay healthy and safe until then."

Chapter 5
May 2340

"Tomb Raiders on the Move"

Erika's return flight delay due to stormy weather worked in her favor. She slept during the first half of the trip back to London, then reviewed her meeting notes before contacting Electra-C.

"I've made so much progress that I plan to launch my first sample collection mission on June 14th. The Robos and I will rent the van and get all the supplies, and we'll keep in constant contact with you in case we run into something we can't handle. And Lily's researching the philosophers you chose for our Philosopher's Council."

"I am pleased with your proactive efficiency. Is there anything else?"

Erika's sense of humor showed in her expression and answer.

"I don't want to give you an information overload by dumping too much at once, so I'll save the rest for later."

Electra-C matched her humor by saying,

"Well then, I'll rest up and be ready when you are," before vanishing.

Lily greeted Erika as soon as she came home, and Erika summarized Monet's meeting. When she finished, Lily said,

"I have a paper for you. Let me give you a copy."

The Philosopher's Council

- Its Purpose: to provide socio-political and ethical recommendations to your Dream Team. It will include Plato, Aristotle, Saint Augustine, Saint Thomas Aquinas, and Spinoza.

- These philosophers constitute the foundation of Classical Western Philosophy, which the American society and its government rely on.
- The Council augments the Dream Team, and the combination will provide additional insights that your socio-political forecasting clients will understand.
- Additional Philosophers to add in the future: Confucius, Siddhartha Gautama (aka the Buddha/the Enlightened One), Muhammad.

Summary of Dream Team Philosophers

Here is a summary of the key philosophical contributions of Plato, Aristotle, Saint Augustine, Saint Thomas Aquinas, and Spinoza, based on classical philosophical frameworks:

- Plato founded the theory of **Forms (Ideas)**, positing that eternal, non-physical abstractions represent true reality, while the physical world is an imperfect reflection. He advocated for **philosopher-kings** in *The Republic*, arguing that rulers with knowledge of the Forms could govern justly. His epistemology centered on **recollection (*anamnesis*)**, suggesting learning is remembering innate knowledge from the soul's pre-existence. Plato also defended the **immortality of the soul** and a tripartite soul structure (reason, spirit, appetite).
- Aristotle rejected Plato's transcendentalism, emphasizing **empirical observation** and **teleology** (purpose-driven nature). He introduced the **four causes** (material, formal, efficient, final) to explain change. For ethics, he defined human flourishing (*eudaimonia*) as the **activity of the soul in accordance with reason**, achievable through virtue. His metaphysics proposed an **Unmoved Mover** as the ultimate cause of motion.
- Saint Augustine synthesized **Christian theology with Platonic thought**, viewing God as the source of eternal Truth. He emphasized **divine grace** for human salvation

and framed history as a struggle between the spiritual *City of God* (spiritual) and earthly *City of Man*.
His *Confessions* explored the **fallen nature of humanity** and the soul's yearning for God.

- Saint Thomas Aquinas integrated **Aristotelian philosophy with Christian doctrine**. His *Summa Theologica* used logical arguments to prove God's existence via the **Five Ways** (e.g., the Unmoved Mover).
He distinguished **faith** (revealed truth) and **reason** (empirical/philosophical truth), asserting their harmony under divine law. Aquinas also systematized **natural law ethics**, positing universal moral principles rooted in human nature.

- Spinoza proposed a **monistic metaphysics** in *Ethics*, declaring that God (*Deus sive Natura*) and Nature are identical. He rejected mind-body dualism, viewing thought and extension as attributes of one substance. His ethics advocated **rational self-determination**, where freedom arises from understanding natural necessity. Spinoza also championed **political secularism**, separating theology from state governance.

Erika skimmed it for two minutes before saying,

"Gads, these look like detailed notes from a philosophy class. I'll study them on my own, and I'm glad there'll be no test. Now let me tell you the details for our first mission to collect DNA samples..."

Erika split the days until Thursday between reviewing with the Robos the mission plan and adding to the Monet meeting notes.
She picked up the van and supplies early Thursday morning and then rested until she and the Robos started driving at 5:30 that evening to Birmingham.
They took the M40, which is the major fast and direct route through the Chilterns and Cherwell Valley, lighted and rarely rural. She glanced out the window as she sat in the middle row while the Robos occupied the first.

We're always in congested traffic, but so far it's OK, no major delay. And the weather's cooperating too. The clouds make it darker sooner, and the forecast says no rain.

Electra-C gave the Robos directions once they exited M40, and Erika listened.

Even Key Hill Cemetery has digitized and computerized data. Electra-C must have hacked into it because she's giving GPS coordinates. I'm glad the Robos know how to use it.

The Robos parked the van in the shadows near Key Hill's main entrance, a little after 8:30, and took everything they needed to the typical wrought iron cemetery gate that looked about ten feet high. They hoisted the ladder, and one of the Robos climbed up and then jumped to the other side.

Carrying the supplies, the other Robo climbed up and dropped them to his partner, and then tied the rope to the top of the ladder. He then motioned for Erika to climb to him, and when she did, he carefully dropped her and her laptop into the arms of his partner before jumping to join them. Then, using the rope, the Robos pulled the ladder over and hid it in the nearby bushes.

Erika traipsed behind the Robos, whose built-in night vision and WI-FI connectivity made it easy to follow Electra-C's directions. She used the flashlight to keep from stumbling, and it helped her see a landscape covered with tombs and gravestones.

When they reached the Martineau gravestone, the Robos used the shovels and earth auger to dig to the coffin, which was buried five feet deep. Then, they used the cordless drill to extract a DNA sample from the body inside. Soon, they were retracing their steps to the entrance after shoveling dirt into the hole.

Erika spotted a roving squad car just before they reached the gate and motioned for the Robos to hoist the ladder after it passed. In less than twenty minutes, they were driving to Winchester Cathedral via M40 and M3 motorways, and when they parked near the walk leading to the entrance, Erika noted the time: almost 11:30 Friday morning.

Unlit at night, the massive, spectacular structure stood in an open, grassy field with a few trees. The Robos drilled out the main entrance door locks and marched to the marble ledger stone marking Jane Austen's burial spot on the floor in the north nave aisle. Then they used the drill, reaching her coffin and retrieving a DNA sample before filling the hole with putty. Even illuminating it with her flashlight, Erika doubted that anyone would notice.

They encountered only one problem on the way out. The replacement door locks didn't fit. Erika didn't worry about it.

The Winchester guards now have a mystery on their hands—why did someone drill out the locks? They might never figure it out.

The trio hustled to the van and started driving at 12:30 on Friday morning to Westminster Abbey, parking at 3 a.m. near the most convenient entrance. The weather had turned rainy and gusty, which Erika liked.

Hardly anyone will be out, and if they are, they won't spot us; the visibility is even less.

Erika gave updated instructions to the Robos.

"Don't worry about replacing the door locks. Just drill out whatever's there and get us in and out as fast as possible. Both of you will drill into different coffins, get samples, and plug the holes with putty. Newton's buried at the Abbey's Scientist Corner, and Darwin's in the north aisle of the nave, which is close to Newton. Now, let's do it."

Even though unlit and obscured by the rain, Erika marveled at what she saw.

It's even more spectacular than Winchester Cathedral. I think Gothic architecture would describe it. The flying buttresses, multiple towers, and carved facades must make it one of England's historical treasures. I bet the interior is just as breathtaking, but there's no time to gawk at it tonight.

Having drilled and plugged only a couple of hours ago, the Robos removed samples even faster. As the trio drove away at 4:30, Erika gave more instructions.

"I'm exhausted, so just drop me off. I'll put the samples in the fridge, and you two park close to the office and stay in the van. When I call you, pick me up and we'll return the van and equipment. Now, drive me to the office."

Erika started to relax while stretching out in the middle row, but flashing lights from behind brought her to attention.

She yelled,

"That has to be a London patrol car. Pull over so we can hear what they say on the loudspeaker, but don't get out until I give the order."

Five minutes later, Erika heard what she expected.

"Turn your engine off. Everyone in the vehicle, get out and stand in front. Keep the headlights on."

Erika told the Robos what to do.

"Stand far enough in front so the bobbies won't turn around. Face them when they reach you, but don't say a word. Now go."

Erika locked the van doors as soon as the Robos left, then positioned herself so she couldn't be seen, even if the bobbies used flashlights, and sure enough, lights and doors rattling on both sides agreed with what she had prepared for.

When the bobbies stopped just out of arm's reach, she heard one of them say,

"Why were you parked at Westminster Abbey? Who are you?"

When they didn't answer, the other said,

"If you won't talk here, we'll take you to the station. Come on, say something."

That's when Erika took action. Carrying a Traser in each hand, she snuck behind the bobbies and gave each a double jolt, which crumpled them lifeless to the pavement. She wrestled each to lie on their backs and then ripped off their body cams before yelling,

"Stay here and make sure they stay down until I get back." Then she ran to the patrol car, removed the incident report, and threw the keys down the sewer grating.

She ran back to the Robos and issued final commands.

"Now, drive me home and do what I already told you. And I know what to do too."

Chapter 6
June 2340

"A Meeting of Brilliant Minds"

Standing nearby, Lily spoke as soon as Erika awoke.

"Last night's Sample Collection Mission must have been cognitively and emotionally exhausting because you slept for seven hours. If you feel ready, why not go for a run to loosen up? I'll have breakfast waiting, and you can eat after showering. Then you can call Electra-C."

"That's the first part of what I had planned for today."

"The weather has cleared, so why not start now?"

"Will do; I'll be back in an hour."

Erika started speaking as soon as Electra-C's avatar appeared.

"Last night's sample-collecting mission went nearly according to plan. We couldn't replace doorknobs, but I don't care. And I saw firsthand how useful the Robo-Soldiers can be on missions and other projects. I'm going to keep these two permanently at the London office."

Erika paused for Electra-C.

"You should also station two at the Bern Deus Lab. Have the A-Team transfer two from the Subterranean Fortress."

"I hadn't thought of that, but it ties in with something I'll do next. I'll have the best Japanese android company build androids that resemble the eight Dream Teamers and the five members of the Philosophers' Council. And when they're built, I'll have the A-Team deliver them to Bern along with the two Robo-Soldiers. All of them will be permanently stationed at the Bern Deus Lab."

"Excellent. And what additional projects are on your list?"

"Well, the very first is to return the van and equipment. Then, I'll order the androids and tell the A-Team. Then, I'll take the samples we collected last night to Bern, which I'll do within the week. Next, I'll plan two additional sample collection missions, one to Paris to get the samples of Simone De Beauvoir and Harriet

Taylor Mill, and the other to Philly and LA to get Einstein's and Richard Feynman's."

"I applaud your thoroughness. Please carry on."

Erika didn't tell Electra-C but was so pleased with her renting the van for last night's mission that she would ask her to rent a car when she was ready to deliver those samples to Bern.

When she ordered the androids, the customer service fellow said they would be ready in four weeks, and Erika said she would give him delivery details if he would call her when they were ready.

With all that taken care of, Erika knew she could relax, so she did that by planning the next two collection missions, preparing for Monet's next meeting, and talking with her London clients.

Erika felt fully energized when the customer service fellow called her, and she told him her favorite delivery company would arrange for pickup. After ending the call, she contacted Electra-C, which agreed to rent a car that the Robos would drive. Erika and Lily would ride in the back seat, talking about upcoming projects, gazing at the scenery, or napping. Then, she told the A-Team what to do.

Erika and her entourage left the next morning. She knew they would arrive before the A-Team, which would give her time to get everything organized.

When they arrived the next day, she and Lily met right away with Indy and Jason-S.

Erika immediately took control of the meeting.

"I'm delivering four DNA samples that I want you to maintain by turning each into its supply, using Indira's DNA processing procedures that you have already set up. Electra-C will guide you to begin growing hermaphroditic, parthenogenic females that I will place at adoption agencies. Is that clear?" Indy and Jason-S nodded, so she continued.

"Good, now I'll tell you about a delivery that should get here in a couple of days. The A-Team will deliver two Robo-Soldiers and thirteen androids. You must set up places for them to stay permanently. The Robo-Soldiers are already trained, but you will follow Electra-C's instructions for first uploading Indira's advanced software into their digital brains. Then, you will follow her instructions for rewiring their digital brains. They are patterned after the 'Brain in a Vat' concept, which she will explain. She will also describe that the androids are grouped into eight that belong to my Dream Team and five that belong to my Philosophers' Council.

That's all you need to know for now. Electra-C will tell you more once they arrive. Are there any questions?"

There were none, so Erika ended the meeting.

"Good. Now start setting up places for all of them to stay."

Erika told Lily to follow Indy and Jason-S so she could see them in action and learn more about the Lab. Erika would join them whenever she took breaks from preparing for the A-Team's arrival.

When the A-Team arrived two days later, Erika gathered everyone in a conference room.

"Here's what's going to happen now. I want the Robo-Soldiers who just arrived to stay with Lily and the Robo's that were already here. She'll show you around the Lab. The thirteen androids that just arrived will get advanced AI software uploaded by Jason and Indy-S. When that's completed, they will use Big-Data to train each according to the person you resemble. They will train you twenty-four-seven, and I will observe periodically. Training ends when I think you're ready for the next step, which I will explain at the next meeting. Now, get started."

The speed and efficiency of the training astonished her.

Indy and Jason-S follow Electra-C's orders perfectly. The androids always follow orders and never need a break. When I think they're ready, I check in with Electra-C to see if she agrees.

Three days later, Erika assembled the androids.

"Congratulations to Indy and Jason-S for completing your training. Eight of you are now ready to become my 'Dream Team' of brilliant minds that I will meet with in person or on the Internet to discuss important topics that my consulting business clients want to know about. And the other five are now my 'Philosophers Council' of the greatest thinkers. They will join our meetings. We will meet whenever I have topics to discuss. All of you are now smarter than mere mortals and will continue training yourselves on Big Data. All of you report to Electra-C, and I talk with her daily. Do you have any questions for me?"

None came, so Erika gave the final instructions.

"You are dismissed. You know what to do, so start doing it."

Staying after all others left, Lily asked,

"What should I do?"

"Pal around with the Dream Team and Philosophers' Council and pick topics of interest to discuss. And while you're doing that, I'll meet again with the director of the Bern adoption agency. I'll tell him that I will soon have orphaned infants ready for adoption, but of course, he'll never know about my partheno-hermaphroditic agenda. And after that, our Robo-Soldiers will drive us back to London."

"What will we do when we get there?"

"Don't you worry. I know, and I'll tell you on the way."

Chapter 7
July 2340

"Time Out for Fun"

Erika decided to hold the next meeting before returning to London, and the results exceeded even her expectations. She ran her socio-political forecasting app and used its output as the meeting's focal point.

Erika sat at a table in the center of a ring of chairs occupied by the thirteen androids, with Indy-S, Jason-S, and Lily observing. Although she controlled the discussion, she let the androids extend the points she introduced and recorded via her laptop's Internet connection the entire ninety-minute discussion.

She ended the meeting by saying,

"In the future, I can run these meetings in person or by setting up a Zoom-type meeting on the Internet. If I'm here, the setup and procedure will be just like today's. If I'm not, Indy and Jason-S will sit at the table, and I will lead it remotely. If there are no questions, everyone is dismissed."

None arose, so Erika and Lily departed for London.

Erika could feel the pressure from all her projects lessen as she continued running more of her Dream Team meetings online, because she could produce better socio-political forecasting reports that she sent to her clients faster than ever. That kept her clients happy, which was the goal of her consulting business.

When Bailey Hughes, her contact for a major London-based drug company, called her a day after meeting with him to discuss his latest customized report, Erika could guess why, but let Bailey lead the conversation.

After exchanging their usual greetings, he said,

"I certainly enjoyed the dancing and concert-going dating we did last year, and I think you did too, but every time I've asked you out since then, you've been too busy. Is that still the situation?"

"I still have a lot going on, but I do have a little more free time. What do you have in mind?"

"Well, since you do political reporting, I thought you might like a guided tour of Parliament on Saturday. It's free, but you have to reserve your spot, so I booked us for it. I'll take you for breakfast, and then we can walk to Westminster Palace. How does that sound?"

"I like it. Why don't you pick me up in front of my office building? Is 9 a.m. good for you?"

"Perfect. I'll see you then."

Erika had to wait only a minute before Bailey arrived and headed them toward a convenient restaurant. He had plenty to say, so Erika did all the listening.

"I'm sure you know that Great Britain's government evolved from a monarchy to its current parliamentary structure, but do you know it doesn't have a constitution?"

"No. what does it have?"

"It has a constitution that is partly written, partly unwritten, and partly based on conventions. This means that while many of the UK's constitutional rules and principles are written in various statutes, court judgments, and treaties, they are not consolidated into a single document."

"So, how is Parliament structured?"

"Like your Congress, it's bicameral. The people elect members of the House of Commons, but members of the House of Lords are appointed for life, on either a political or non-political basis. And Parliament is led by a prime minister who is appointed by Parliament, which means the prime minister usually comes from the political party having the most members."

"What role does the Monarchy play?"

"Today, the King and Queen are strictly ceremonial, although Parliament will listen to them."

"I'm learning a lot. Keep going."

"Parliament meets in Westminster Palace. The surrounding area is called Whitehall, which is a metonym for the government, just like the White House is for yours."

"Why the name Whitehall?"

"The Palace at Whitehall was named for the white stone used to construct it, and today it's both a street and the area around Westminster Palace."

Bailey glanced at his cell phone before continuing.

"You now know more about the British government than most Americans. I'll tell you more about the area as we hike to Westminster. Are you ready?"

"Yes, let's go."

The cool, sunny morning made for pleasant walking. As they walked past 10 Downing Street, Bailey said,

"This is where the Prime Minister lives. It's not so impressive on the outside. The white-framed door and black wrought-iron fence are pretty common in the area, but the interior is another matter. I've taken the tour, which displays British political history and taste. I'll take you sometime, if you like."

Erika nodded, and Bailey kept talking all the way to Westminster.

The tour took three hours, and it impressed Erika as much as Bailey's build-up had indicated. As they filtered past Parliament chambers, the guide said,

"We could view a debate if Parliament were in session today, but that doesn't happen very often on Saturday. However, you can watch sessions online during the week."

After exiting Westminster, Bailey began leading them through another street in Whitehall.

"We could stop for lunch and then go to a nearby museum if you like."

Erika stopped and replied.

"Thanks for the offer, but I think I'll walk home. I have some project work waiting."

Bailey couldn't hide his disappointment, which showed in his voice, too.

"I understand, but I have some ideas for next weekend, so please keep that in mind. Is it OK if I call you Thursday evening?"

"That'll be fine, and thanks again for today."

Erika returned his hug and let him kiss her on the cheek before they went their separate ways.

Everything went according to plan the following week, so Erika knew what to say when she recognized Bailey's voice when he called Thursday evening.

"I've had a good week, and I hope you have too, and if you're available on Saturday, how would you like to see a Shakespeare play at the Royal Shakespeare Theatre in Stratford-upon-Avon?"

"That sounds like fun. Where's Stratford?"

"It's 110 miles northwest of London, so it'll take us about three hours to get there. I'll pick you up at four and have snacks in the car so we can drive nonstop."

"That's great. I'll be waiting outside my office building. Should I wear anything in particular?"

"I'll be in business-casual, but you look spectacular in anything, so you decide. Cheerio."

Bailey regaled her with some Shakespearean background while driving.

"People around the world love Shakespeare's plays, but no place more than England. Have you read some of them?"

"Just the popular ones. I covered Hamlet, Othello, Macbeth, and King Lear in a high school English course."

"I took a Shakespeare course in college. The four you mentioned are his most famous tragedies. The professor grouped his plays into three categories—the kind you just mentioned, histories like 'King John' and Henry the Eighth', and comedies like 'The Taming of the Shrew' and 'Much Ado About Nothing.' These categories are based on the overall tone, themes, and structure of the plays, as established in the First Folio of 1623. But there are other categories too.

"We'll be seeing my favorite, 'The Tempest,' which is categorized as one of his romance plays. While it contains elements of tragedy and comedy, its focus on themes of forgiveness, reconciliation, and the supernatural, along with its happy ending, aligns it with the romance genre."

"What's it about?"

"It tells the story of Prospero, the rightful Duke of Milan, who was displaced by his brother Antonio and exiled to a remote island with his daughter Miranda. Using magic, Prospero conjures a tempest that shipwrecks his enemies, including Antonio and Alonso, the King of Naples, near his island. Through a series of events involving love, deception, and manipulation, Prospero seeks revenge and ultimately regains his dukedom, while also orchestrating the marriage of his daughter to Alonso's son, Ferdinand."

"You must have been a brilliant student to remember all that."

"I was, and I can tell you even more. In the 'Cinema and Media Studies' course I took, I learned that many movies use Shakespeare's plays for plots. Do you like to watch movies?"

"When I have the time."

"Well, since you don't and I do, you probably never heard of 'The Lion King,' which is loosely based on 'Hamlet,' or 'West Side Story,' which is based on 'Romeo and Juliet.' And my absolute favorite is the iconic sci-fi classic, 'Forbidden Planet,' which is based on what we'll see tonight. Even when compared to today's marvelous special effects, the movie is breathtaking. If you like tonight's performance, I'll rent it and we can watch it sometime."

Bailey kept talking until he parked in a grassy field near the tourist area and then led them to the theatre. By the time they entered, Erika knew more about Shakespeare than she would ever need. She even knew that his grave contains only his body. Archaeologists have concluded via X-ray scanning that his head is somewhere else.

For the next three hours, the stage setting and the magic of the actors drew Erika into the story. As they left the theatre, she said,

"What a wonderful experience. I'm now ready to watch 'Forbidden Planet' with you. Say, why don't I buy us dessert before we drive back to London?"

Grabbing her hand, Bailey joined a merry crowd heading toward the tourist area and picked a place he had heard about. As soon as they entered, Erika felt like she had just stepped back in time, but waited until he chose a place before saying,

"I've never been in anything like this before. What would you call it?"

"It's a traditional alehouse. Alehouses were central to social life in Shakespeare's time, and this one has an interior like then. That's why we're sitting on stools at a bench near a brick fireplace embedded in timbered and plastered walls, but the lightning's brighter, the floor's smoother, and I guarantee the food is thoroughly contemporary. Here comes our waitress with the menu."

She looked like she had just stepped out of a play, and after she left, Erika said,

"Do you suppose Shakespeare would have thought that people would still be watching his plays over five hundred years after he died?"

"He might have. Besides being a storytelling genius, he understood human nature, and it turns out that people love listening to how his characters speak and what they do. And even in Shakespeare's time, people loved to travel and listen to stories. Chaucer's Canterbury Tales and Boccaccio's Decameron illustrate this."

Just before the ice cream sundaes arrived, Erika said,

"Do you suppose Shakespeare would have guessed that Stratford would become a tourist town? All the people working here can thank Shakespeare for their jobs."

Bailey dug into his hot fudge sundae instead of answering the question, but he did ask one when they left.

"It's pretty late for driving back to London, so why don't we stay the night and do some sightseeing tomorrow? There are plenty of bed-and-breakfast places, and I packed toothbrushes and paste."

Erika said,

"OK, but I don't know you well enough to spend the night in the same bed, so how about I rent a room?"

"That'll work."

After retrieving his bag from the car, Bailey took her hand and walked them toward the B&B lane. And when they said goodnight,

Erika rewarded him with warm hugs and lingering kisses on this magically glorious midsummer night.

Bailey joined after breakfast a guided tour that started at Shakespeare's grave and then wound through the nearby streets before going down a lane lined with Cotswald cottages whose exterior matched the timbered and plastered interior of last night's alehouse.

The guide mentioned that the Cotswalds region is known for its picturesque rolling hills and outstanding natural beauty. By the time the tour ended, Erika felt pleasantly tired and ready for a snack. Afterwards, when they reached the car, she stretched her arms overhead before saying,

"I think we're both touristed out. I'm all listened out, and you must be talked out, so I'm going to nap on the drive back to London. Wake me when we get to my place.

When Bailey did that by kissing his sleeping beauty on her forehead after tousling her hair, Erika said,

"You certainly know how to pick fun places for weekends. What do you have in mind for next Saturday?"

"Let me surprise you when I call Thursday evening."

Erika said,

"I'll be ready," before giving him one last kiss and then dashing into her office building. Bailey followed her with his eyes while marveling with surprise at his stupendous luck, hoping for more next weekend.

All next week, Erika made sure all projects proceeded according to plan, so when Bailey called, she was ready.

She enjoyed listening to his breezy small talk, and when he asked about her week, she said,

"Everything's under control, so I'm ready to take you up on your Saturday surprise."

"That sounds delightful. I thought we would go sightseeing and boating near Dover."

"I've heard of it but don't know much, other than it has white cliffs."

"Not to worry. I'll tell you on the drive. Dover's right on the English Channel, seventy-eight miles southwest of London, so we'll have about two hours to chat."

"What should I wear?"

"Typical tourist clothes for hiking about on the cliffs and being in the water. There's plenty to see and do, so why don't you pack a bag for two days? We can do more on Sunday if you're having fun."

"What time will you pick me up?"

"I think 8 a.m. will be ideal. We'll have a bite to eat when we get there and then dive into the action at noon."

"My choice of words works. I said I'm ready to take you up on your Saturday surprise, and you must be ready to take us up somewhere, if we're diving into the action."

"How clever of you. We shall continue on Saturday. Cheers until then."

As soon as Bailey disconnected, a devilish thought brought out Erika's wicked smile.

Bailey's planned an action-packed weekend, and I know what to pack to keep him motivated… maybe he can do the same for me… we'll just have to wait and see…

After jumping into the car and planting a cherry-red flavored kiss on Bailey's lips, Erika knew it had the desired effect when a smile emerged along with words whose tone matched his animated expression as he started driving.

"I know this will be a special weekend. Not only will you see Dover from a unique vantage point, but you'll learn significant facts about the place. You'll see Dover Castle and the city from high above and hear about its significant military roles in World War One and Two."

"So, what does the place look like?"

"Dover has a bustling port, largely because it's England's closest point to France, and its chalky white cliffs, dropping dramatically to the English Channel, stretch for miles. The area retains its historical charm with remnants of Roman and Napoleonic fortifications. The breathtaking coastal scenery and rolling countryside are perfect for walking, which means were likely to see lots of hikers because of the weekend's warm, sunny weather.

"What about Dover Castle?"

"Enclosed within fortified walls, it looms over the north side of the city. It has secret World War II tunnels and an underground hospital. We can take a guided tour and combine it with a visit to the Canterbury Cathedral if we stay the entire weekend."

"What's the rest of its military history?"

"During the Dunkirk evacuation, British and French troops fled from the beaches and harbor of Dunkirk to England. Most of the rescued troops landed in Dover. And Dover played a crucial role in the D-Day deception, specifically through Operation Fortitude South, which aimed to mislead the Germans about the true location of the invasion. Dover's strategic location and the tunnels beneath Dover Castle became a key area for creating a false impression of a buildup of Allied forces preparing to attack the Pas-de-Calais region, rather than Normandy."

"You know so much. Did you take a History of World War II course in college?"

"I took several History of England courses that included lots of English wars. Did you take any History of the United States courses that might have included its military history?"

"No, but what can you tell me?"

"The world owes the United States for its money and manpower that ultimately defeated Germany not once, but twice. Likewise, for neutralizing Russia and North Korea by waging the Korean War. It also defended democracy by defeating Russia in the Cold War, and it kept oil flowing from the Middle East by defeating Iraq in two major conflicts—the Persian Gulf War that started in 1990, and the Iraq War that began in 2003.

"But since then, the United States has de-emphasized globalization and its role in defending other nations. And today, with the U.S.-Russian Alliance in control of Washington, other nations, though they still like the American people, don't like the United States."

"You know more about U.S. military history than I do. What else should I know?"

By the time they reached Dover, Erika knew more than enough for her consulting role. After having lunch, Bailey drove to the harbor area that featured parasailing charters. After connecting with one that would leave in fifteen minutes with two other couples, they changed into swimwear.

Bailey's eyes devoured Erika when she emerged from the changing area wearing a cherry-red thong bikini. His facial expression and voice showed glowing admiration.

"You could model old bathrobes and guys would still follow you, hoping to see what's underneath."

Erika's coy look came with her words.

"Why, thank you. Perhaps you'll be the one, but let's go parasailing first."

The three couples sat at the stern, just in front of the two-seat bench tethered to the tow rope and its support harness attached to the parasail. As the boat motored out of the harbor, the sound of the engines and the water rushing past made conversation difficult, so everyone withdrew into their thoughts. The warm sun and cool onshore winds combined with a tangy ocean fragrance, bringing back memories.

I recall parasailing in Florida with my dearly departed Terri. I loved her so. And I'm beginning to love Bailey, but in a different way. Friendship and unconditional love were my feelings for Terri, but romance and erotic love are my feelings for Bailey. It's too soon to tell him, but maybe I'll drop hints tonight. We shall see…"

The skipper idled the engine so the instructor could explain what would happen next. Then he asked each couple to tell their parasailing experience. After that, they drew straws to determine the order. Erika liked theirs.

How nice; we go second, which'll give me a chance to see what the boat does and how the parasail behaves.

Forty-five minutes later, Erika and Bailey buckled into their harnesses, and the boat charged ahead, catapulting them into the cloudless sky.

The soaring and swooping thrilled all her senses. She lost track of time, but suddenly she saw a drone swoop toward them, firing bullets that cut the towline. The parasail soared even higher and veered toward shore.

Once over the grassy fields, Erika spotted people hiking below. *We're so high that they look like a column of ants… oh, dear Jeezus, the drone's coming at us again…*

This time, it blasted holes in the parasail. Parasail, harness, and its occupants plunged toward a crash landing on the grass. Erika folded her legs to protect them from the impact, but when looking at Bailey, she saw he hadn't. She screamed and pointed, but Bailey didn't react in time.

After everything bounced to a stop, Erika unfastened her harness and then reached to help Bailey, but the condition of his leg, his glassy eyes, and motionless body warned her. So, after standing, she spied a group of people running toward her. She ran toward them, and when they were close enough, yelled,

"My partner's in shock from a broken leg. Call an ambulance."

One raced across the grass an unknown number of minutes later. The EMTs loaded Bailey onto a stretcher, and they raced away, with Erika riding next to him.

She stood next to him while the ER doctor made his diagnosis. Bailey was now conscious and felt no pain, but he still looked confused, so she said,

"I'll be a combination ombudsman-caregiver for my partner, Bailey Hughes. Our parasail crash-landed hard enough to break his leg. What other damage did it do?"

"It's good you're here. Well, it gave him a severe compound fracture of the left tibia. The bones are protruding. We'll stop the bleeding, clean the wound, and then get our orthopedic surgeon to insert pins and screws to immobilize it. The entire procedure will take at least four hours. You can stay in the waiting area, and I'll have a nurse give you a uniform to wear."

"Thank you. I'm beat, so I'll nap. Please wake me after you put him in a recovery room."

After the surgeon did that, he took her to Bailey so both of them could hear the results.

"The procedure was successful. You're out of immediate danger. I've put a brace on your leg, and you can go home, but you'll need to be in a wheelchair until your regular physician reviews what we did and how you're progressing. We'll give you a wheelchair to take home. Your physician can expense it using your health insurance plan. Where is your car parked?"

"At Dover Harbor, near the parasail charter company. I'm sure it'll still be open because of my accident."

"One of our ambulances will take you. I'll give your partner a folder with all the information your doctor will need to help plan your recovery. So, if you and your partner have no further questions, you are good to go."

Erika spoke before Bailey could.

"Thank you, doctor, but I do have a final question. Do you think Bailey's football career is over?"

When seeing the humor in her eyes, he said,

"If he's smart enough to know ahead of time where the ball's going, maybe he can become a goalkeeper."

"Oh, he's plenty smart, and I have a forecasting business. We can think about working together during his recovery."

The parasail charter company people were relieved when Bailey and Erika returned and had all their belongings waiting, even refunding what they had paid. After loading the wheelchair into the trunk, their instructor helped Bailey stretch out in the back seat. Before driving away, Erika said,

"Although Bailey's parasailing career has come to an end, we'll have to watch the news to see if he made the headlines. May I call you tomorrow to find out?"

"Please do; here's our cell phone number. I imagine you'll have your hands full tomorrow."

"I always do, but I'm ready to make room for Bailey."

Bailey roused himself enough to say,

"Me too, you too," before Erika, with eyes shining bright, sped away into this singular night.

Chapter 8
August 2340

"Once Upon a Time in America"

Thanks to his doctor and health insurance, Bailey had recovered enough by the end of July to return to work. Insurance covered the cost of a healthcare aide and a physical therapist who treated him at home, and his company hired a personal assistant who drove him to and from work during the week.

All this obviated Erika's role as his caregiver, but she volunteered to take over on weekends by staying the weekend and doing whatever might be needed, such as shopping for groceries, preparing meals, taking him out in his wheelchair, and binge-watching movies or online series.

She rented "Forbidden Planet" as soon as Bailey adjusted to his new lifestyle, and they watched it on Saturday evening, two weeks after the accident. He was the first to speak after it ended.

"I never tire of watching it. Unlike most sci-fi movies today, viewers don't have to suspend disbelief to enjoy it, because it begins 200,000 years in the future. The advanced race of people who vanished from Altair IV was called the Krell. It was an ancient, brilliant, and technologically advanced civilization that mysteriously perished 200,000 years before the events of the movie. This lets viewers assume that if you project our current technology that far into the future, what you see in the special effects is plausible. Perhaps the spaceship didn't travel faster than the speed of light. Maybe the crew had an advanced form of NASA's suspension pods that put astronauts in suspended animation while traveling millions of miles through our solar system."

Erika added more.

"I particularly liked their brain-booster teaching machine, which eliminated the need for schools and teachers. We don't have brain-booster machines today, but students can take college courses and even earn degrees online. Say, do you take the brain-boosting vitamins your pharmaceutical company makes?"

"No, clinical studies show placebos work just as well."

"Well, how'd you like the machine that could give physical form and life to their subconscious desires? In a single night, the machine unleashed these 'Monsters from the Id,' as they are called in the film, and they destroyed the entire Krell race. Do you think this machine is an analogy for the Atomic Bomb?"

"What accurate insights you have. According to my cinema professor, it is widely interpreted that way by sci-fi lovers. The movie also asks this question—are our Freudian Ids, which come from our ape-like emotional-brains, ready for that kind of increase in power? And although the movie has a partially happy ending—the spaceship gets far enough away to avoid destruction when the planet blows up, and the captain, who has romantic intentions for the daughter of Morbius and vice versa, takes her with him—Morbius destroys the machine and blows up the planet, which reinforces the cautionary message about the dangers of technological hubris and the potential for self-destruction inherent in technologies like the atomic bomb."

"You certainly know your sci-fi, but consider this. Our generation has grown up with fears different than the atomic bomb. We have global pandemics, terrorism, and climate change. Ensuing generations have grown up with their own fears--climate change and AI in particular are upending life across the globe."

"Right you are, and I would add fear of the U.S.-Russian Alliance to the list. But I would also add three additional sci-fi future projection fears—genetic engineering, cloning from the DNA of extraordinary people who are now dead, and Androids running amok. I read a newspaper article about a nighttime break-in at Westminster Abbey. The security guards initially found nothing missing or out of place, but the search continued until they discovered that holes had been drilled into the coffins of Darwin and Einstein to remove tissue samples from which DNA could be extracted. Do you suppose—," Erika cut him off mid-sentence.

"I wouldn't suppose anything about that, but what tidbits do you have about energy?"

"Here's one that only hardcore sci-fi lovers will know—the Kardashev scale. It's a method for classifying civilizations based on their level of technological advancement, specifically their energy consumption. The Soviet astronomer Nikolai Kardashev proposed it in the mid-1960s. The scale categorizes civilizations into three main types, with Type I utilizing all the energy of its planet, Type II harnessing the power of its star, and Type III controlling the energy of its galaxy. I'm certain you know where our civilization fits."

"We're Type II, and since you made some points regarding civilization, I can extend them. Even 200,000 years into the future, the brilliant Krell's genetic material never evolved past what our emotional persona is today. Their 'Monsters from the Id' were like ours, which says the Krell had all the emotional flaws that people have today. How do you like that?"

"That's a novel insight. Can you—"

Erika cut him off again.

"Yes, I can extend it further into what you taught me about America's military history. Here's how. A civilization evolves too, largely controlled by its government's socio-politics. The World used to love America, but today it doesn't because of the control exercised by the U.S.-Russian Alliance. America has evolved to a worse state. I've read articles that say America's government is evolving backward, or devolving. Animals evolve only forward—either they improve or go extinct. But societies and civilizations can evolve forward or backward."

Erika had said all she wanted and waited for Bailey.

"The skills you developed as a reporter combine with your cleverness to make what you say relevant. Whew, I'm ready for a break. Did you buy ice cream?"

"I also bought fudge topping, so hot fudge sundaes will be coming your way with no further delay…"

When Erika started staying with Bailey once or twice a week, her romantic feelings deepened, and time spent with him helped her client work. She became an expert at running online meetings with her Dream Team as well as doing the same with her clients.

However, when ending the latest one with her favorite Washington client at the end of August, Monet made a request that would cause a change for the next one.

"My Matriarchate Party congresswomen's group is ready for our next session, and its leading spokesperson has requested that you be present. Will you join us?"

"What's the date?"

"We're still finalizing it, but it will be in the third week of September."

"I'll be there if you call me several days in advance."

"I will. Thank you for being so flexible."

"Of course, I am. You're my number one client. You can count on me to be ready. Bye for now."

Telling Bailey after ending the call, he said,

"That's almost three weeks away, and at the rate I'm recovering, I should be fine on my own. But I'll miss you while you're gone."

"Me too, you too, but counselors say time away heightens our appreciation for one another."

"That's true, and I listened to a motivational speaker who said people can adjust to anything if they role-play it in advance. So, now that I know what you're planning, I'll be doubly fine…"

Erika's daily work schedule balanced running reports for clients, preparing for Monet's upcoming meeting, and going for a run when she needed a break from thinking too long about upcoming projects.

Having Emailed Chelsea's latest report last week, Chelsea's call surprised her. After exchanging their typical greetings, Chelsea said,

"I've got some questions about a couple of the points you made. Could we meet at my office this week?"

Erika faked being pressed for time by saying,

"Let me check my schedule," and continued a minute later.

"How about Friday at 10 a.m.?"

"That's the day after tomorrow, and that'll work. See you then."

Erika returned to prepping for Monet's meeting but made little progress, so she went for a run ninety minutes later. Several miles into it, a sudden inspiration came.

I have something that both Monet and Chelsea can use, and it'll lighten my load even more. I'll research it after lunch with Bailey, then outline it and start writing it tomorrow.

Bailey noticed that Erika was even more focused than usual and asked at dinner,

"You must be having fun on one of your projects. What have you been doing?"

"Outlining a story for Chelsea."

"What's it about?"

"I'll tell you when I'm finished."

"When will that be?"

"She and I are meeting at her office on Friday, and I must finish it before Monet's DC meeting because the two are interrelated."

"How efficient, but I would expect no less. After all, you are the multi-tasker par excellence…"

After dispatching with ease the answers to Chelsea's questions, Erika began weaving a story that would draw Chelsea in.

"I have an idea for interviews you can conduct with the American public that will be one-of-a-kind that your boss will love. Would you like to hear it?"

"Of course. With that kind of teaser intro, who wouldn't?"

"OK, here goes. Once upon a time in America, a Frenchman interviewed American citizens to find out why the country embraced democracy so quickly, but France, in particular, as well as other European countries, struggled to do so. Who is that fellow?"

"You're talking about Alexis de Tocqueville, the French political scientist and historian best known for his book, 'Democracy in America,' which he wrote after visiting the U.S. in the early 1830s."

"Do you remember the key points?"

Chelsea's perplexed look preceded what she said.

"Are you kidding? Hardly anyone does. Where's all this going?"

"I'll make the connection in a minute. Just bear with me. First, here are the major points. The will of the American people is the driving force that shapes its government, society, and institutions, and the citizens used democracy to balance liberty and equality, but they also understood the damage the tyranny of the majority can do. That's why Americans today volunteer and want social mobility with no elitist groups. After all, the United States had just won the Revolutionary War, defeating the ultimate elitist group, Great Britain's monarchy. And Americans are action-oriented and pragmatic.

"Now, here's the connection. I'm going to a Matriarchate Party's private meeting in a couple of weeks. If you come with me, you'll get a behind-the-curtain look at what it's doing to redeem the American Dream. You already know that its manifesto supports democratic and traditional American values, supports DEI initiatives blended with meritocracy, and is dedicated to isocracy, a form of government invented by ancient Greek philosophers in which all citizens have equal political power.

"And after the meeting, we can travel to the most influential American cities and conduct person-on-the-street interviews. I'll pay all travel expenses. All you pay for are your meals and hotel rooms. And when we get back to London, you and your boss can write an exclusive article that you can summarize on a new broadcast. Do you think you can get your boss to buy in?"

"Wow, this is dynamite. He'll love it."

"Great. I'll call so you know when we'll leave, and I'll leave it to you and your boss to contact the major papers in New York, Philadelphia, Miami, Atlanta, Chicago, Houston, Dallas, Denver, Los Angeles, and San Francisco to arrange for interview crews. Your boss can pay for them."

"I'll have everything set when you call."

Rising to leave, Erika said,

"I will too."

Calling the A-Team as soon as she returned to the office, Erika started the conversation with her usual contact.

"I need you to take me and a client on a trip that starts at my London office. Her office is nearby, so after you pick up both of us, you'll take us to Washington, DC for a meeting. After the meeting, you'll take us, in this order, to New York, Philadelphia, Miami, Atlanta, Chicago, Houston, Dallas, Denver, Los Angeles, and San Francisco. After we conduct interviews, you'll take us back to our offices in London. I'll call you as soon as I know when we leave for DC. Do you have any questions?"

"Ah so, Ms. Erika. We be ready when you call."

Erika and Chelsea were the first to arrive at Monet's meeting being held at the Zimbabwean Embassy on Thursday, September 26th. Erika introduced Chelsea and explained that she would like to know more about the Matriarchate Party's views on current problems facing the U.S. and current problems facing democracy across the globe, but she would disclose no confidential information. Afterward, the two of them would conduct person-on-the-street interviews at major U.S. cities regarding their concerns.

Monet said,

"Since she is a London-based reporter for the New York Times, I imagine an article and a news broadcast will follow. They can help suggest to listeners why citizens everywhere should support the Matriarchate Party."

Electra said,

"That's the main reason she's here. I'll let you introduce her to the group."

"Yes. Let's go to the conference room. The congresswomen will be here in thirty minutes."

Erika sat and listened while Chelsea took notes. After the meeting adjourned at 4 p.m., Erika and Chelsea met in Monet's office before departing.

Erika let Chelsea speak for both of them.

"This has been a super-educational experience for me. Let me show you how I organized my notes."

She slid them across the desk to Monet. Erika leaned forward to read them.

Current Problems Facing the U.S.

1. Economic Concerns
- Inflation and Health Care Affordability, which affects lower and middle-income families
- Federal Budget Deficit-Cutting, which the Current Admin does by axing social welfare programs

2. Political and Governance Issues
- Money in Politics, which buys favors for the Elites.
- Partisan Gridlock among the four political parties.
- U.S.-Russian Alliance controls the Current Admin.

2. Social and Policy Challenges
- Gun Violence.
- Drug Addiction.
- Declining Moral Values.
- Immigration Policy Proposals that threaten mass deportation of groups that don't like the current President.

3. Technology.
- Artificial Intelligence (AI).
- Cybersecurity.

4. Miscellaneous
- Climate Change

Current Problems Facing Democracy Around the Globe

1. Global Democratic Decline and Rise of Autocracy.

2. Erosion of Civil Liberties and Political Rights. The number of autocracies has now surpassed the number of democracies
- Further autocracy risks are deepening, with countries regressing to more closed and repressive forms of government.

- Freedoms such as credible elections, economic equality, and press freedom are weakening.
- Actions such as mass pardons for rioters, replacement of key officials with loyalists, and restrictions on freedom of expression and academic inquiry have raised alarms about democratic backsliding.

3. Rise of Authoritarian and Populist Movements

4. Disinformation, Election Manipulation, and Polarization.

5. Weakening of Institutional Checks and Rule of Law

6. Global Geopolitical Volatility and Armed Conflict
- Regional conflicts are further destabilizing democratic governance and international cooperation.

7. Backsliding on Rights and Social Progress

Matriarchate Party Concerns

1. The White House Fake News about the Party.
2. Recruiting male members of Congress to join us.
3. Convincing Voters to vote for our candidates.
4. Defending the Party and its members from physical attacks.

Monet spoke first five minutes later.

"You listen and summarize well. I have nothing to add," but Erika did.

"Chelsea should include the Matriarchate Party Concerns. I'll give them to her, and when Chelsea writes her 'person-on-the-street article' that'll be used in a broadcast, I'll help her spin it in the Matriarchate Party's favor."

"That should do it. Anything else before you leave?"

Chelsea surprised Erika by saying,

"While I'm in Washington, how can I take a tour of Arlington National Cemetery?"

Erika jumped in.

"Why do you want to tour a cemetery?"

"Because I've toured the most well-known cemetery associated with the D-Day invasion in Normandy, the American Cemetery and Memorial, and want to compare it with Arlington."

Erika looked at Monet while saying,

"Do you suppose Alonzo could take us?"

"Yes. He took me on the guided tour years ago. When would you like to go?"

"Tomorrow, if that's OK with him."

"It will be. He'll pick you up at your hotel at 10 a.m. He'll call your cell phone number when he's in front of the hotel. Where are you staying?"

"At the Washington Hilton."

"Alonzo will be there on time."

As she rose to leave, Erika reached to shake Monet's hand before saying,

"On behalf of Chelsea and myself, I thank you and Alonzo. I'll call you when we get back to London."

After having a light dinner at the hotel, Erika told Chelsea they could relax that night because they would have the entire weekend to prepare for the next leg of their trip. Then she called the A-Team to arrange for their Saturday morning pick-up, and afterward she went to the fitness center; Chelsea went to bed.

Alonzo picked them up right on time. After Erika made the introductions and Chelsea added her thanks, he said,

"The cemetery's nearby. It's on the east side of the Potomac River, just across from the Lincoln Memorial. I'll let the tour guides tell you all the rest as the tram takes us around."

The cloudless sky and tree-lined drives passing fields of immaculately manicured grass holding geometrically perfect rows of white rectangular headstones put Erika in a reflective mood. She paid enough attention to the guides but also to her thoughts.

What I'm seeing and hearing stirs my soul, making me appreciate the sacrifices these brave soldiers made for America. And the changing of the guards ceremony at the Tomb of the Unknown Soldier needed no words to stir my emotions even more.
I'll tell Chelsea to treat Alonzo to lunch and say more.

Erika didn't need to say anything to Chelsea. She volunteered to treat, and Alonzo knew just the place to chat about what they had just seen.

Erika did all the listening to the conversation, which Chelsea started.

"When we drove across the Potomac River, I could see that the cemetery is surrounded on its other sides by such a beautifully lush forest situated on gently rolling hills. And now I know that the Union soldiers established it during the Civil War when burying their fallen comrades on Confederate General Robert E. Lee's plantation, which he named Arlington. The plantation house sits atop the crest of a hill overlooking the cemetery, the Lincoln Memorial and Bridge, and much of Washington. It's an honor for anyone who has served in the Military to be buried here. Are you a veteran?"

"I'm a special forces ex-Navy SEAL, but I'm not planning to be buried here, at least not anytime soon. What special forces does your country have?"

"Great Britain's special forces are collectively called the United Kingdom Special Forces, or UKSF. It includes air and boat service, but I don't know the rest."

"According to what I'm hearing, they're gonna have to build themselves up because the White House is gonna cut back even further on funding for weapons and soldiers to help defend the EU."

"I learned more about that possibility at Monet's meeting. Say, if you don't mind my asking, what's the connection between you and Monet?"

"After being discharged from the SEALs, I started a logistics and security services business. Monet contacted me to provide the Zimbabwean Embassy with them."

"I hope the U.S.-Russian Alliance doesn't cause disruptions that will bring you into the fray…"

When Chelsea and Alonzo ran out of items to talk about, Erika said,

"It's time to get back to the living. Please take us to the hotel."

"Will do, and thanks to Chelsea, sometimes there is a free lunch."

As soon as the duo entered their hotel room, Erika said,

"You can do more local sightseeing, but I'm going to the fitness center. The pressure's off tonight because we have the entire weekend to prepare for person-on-the-street interviewing. Why not watch local news and TV shows this evening to see what's on people's minds?"

"I might, or I might use my meeting notes to start writing an article. Both options are fine by me …"

Everything on the interviewing leg of the trip rolled out according to all the plans Erika and Chelsea put in place. The weather in all cities cooperated, adding to the A-Team's fast and efficient travel procedures. It also helped the experienced interview crews set up and shoot because the passers-by enjoyed being out in the sun, and once Chelsea explained why she wanted to interview them, they were happy to oblige.

By the time the return flight to London reached cruising altitude, Erika and Chelsea had the luxury of decompressing completely from the accumulated stress. After snacking and relaxing for several hours, both of them looked ready for Erika to outline what they would do when back in London. Erika's voice sounded as stress-free as she looked.

"You've already made a good start on the article, and from what the interviewees said, their concerns jibe with the concerns identified by the congresswomen. Which ones in particular did you notice?"

"Everyone's concerned about keeping their jobs and getting paid enough to avoid living paycheck to paycheck. Many of them mentioned being angry at the budget cuts targeting social programs they rely on, which adds to their fears about the U.S.-Russian Alliance pushing people aside in favor of the elites. And they're mad at Congress for playing too much partisan politics."

Chelsea paused for Erika.

"I would add that most of them worry little about issues outside the country, but they do hope the current administration will help the European Union defend itself. And everyone likes the idea of the Matriarch Party."

"Did you pick up on the concern of those with children regarding the future of education? They're worried that the government's cutting funding to education and AI software, which is getting even smarter, will make the skills their kids are learning obsolete."

"I didn't. You won't need much help from me on either Monet's paper or your broadcast script, so I can concentrate on what I need to do next."

"I imagine one of the items will be additional Matriarchate Party ideas for the November elections."

"That's one, and I want to multi-task it with other projects to conserve my time and energy."

"I've noticed how you always combine what you can. I'll do the same in the future."

"Good, well that's enough talking for now. I'm going to think about multi-tasking while I fall asleep."

As Erika withdrew into herself, a succession of random thoughts led to one that startled her.

Aha…I've got an idea that will let me multi-task my most important projects…I'll get busy on them tomorrow.

Chapter 9
August 2340

"The Multi-Tasker Plans Ahead"

The next morning, Erika was about to dive into her two most important projects when her cellphone chimed. Recognizing Bailey's caller I.D., she answered, and after exchanging greetings, let him lead the discussion.

"I'm happy you've returned. I missed you. How did Monet's meeting go?"

"Even better than I had hoped. I came away with more work, so I'll be busy scoping it out, but I know what to do. And how are you?"

"Doing fine. Will you have time to come over this weekend?"

"No, but I'll clear my schedule for the next. And I'm expecting to be surprised by what you arrange for us."

"I already have several options. We'll discuss them when I call next Thursday, so get busy getting the work done."

After he ended the call, Erika called Chelsea, whose voice bubbled with enthusiasm.

"I'm making great progress on both writing my article and making a composite video of the interviews. When it's done, I'll write my broadcast script and have the boss slot me on the news. How're you doing?"

"I'm ready to start, and you could do me a big favor by giving me copies of your video and article. When might you have them?"

"Next week, Wednesday, or even sooner. How about I call, and you can come to my office?"

"Wonderful. Let's stay healthy and safe til then."

Erika paced herself by alternating consulting work and combining her two crucial projects. When Chelsea called early Wednesday afternoon, Erika dashed to her office. They reviewed the article first, then Chelsea played the video.

When finished, Chelsea said nothing, waiting for Erika, who didn't disappoint.

"You should get a promotion. These are just what I need. May I take them with me?"

"You bet; let me know how it all works out."

Erika said,

"I will," before hurrying away.

When Bailey called Thursday evening, Erika had already practiced what to say. After he asked how her week had gone, she said,

"I made enough progress to spend some time with you this weekend. What have you lined up?"

"I thought you might enjoy attending a lecture at the British Museum titled "An Eclectic History of England Now that you're living here, you should know more about its history."

"What time should I get to your place?"

"It starts at 3 p.m., so if you get here by one, we'll take the Tube and have time for me to explain the notes I compiled for you while having a snack at the Museum's cafeteria."

"Why do I need notes?"

"So you can keep up. Most people in the audience are native Brits, who know more about England than any history or philosophy professor running any English history or philosophy courses you may have taken."

"I stand corrected. I'll be at your place right on time."

Having already mastered shuttling Bailey around on the Tube, she soaked in the surroundings while listening to his directions.

The cool sunny weather adds to my enjoyment, wheeling past the Bloomsbury neighborhood's blend of bustling urban traffic and greenery. And the buildings leading up to it have traditional historic architecture.

Erika wheeled Bailey down the cafeteria's serving line a little after 2 p.m. After he paid, she pushed him to an out-of-the-way table, unloaded the trays, and sat next to him. They ate for only a minute before Bailey placed the notes in front of her.

A History of England

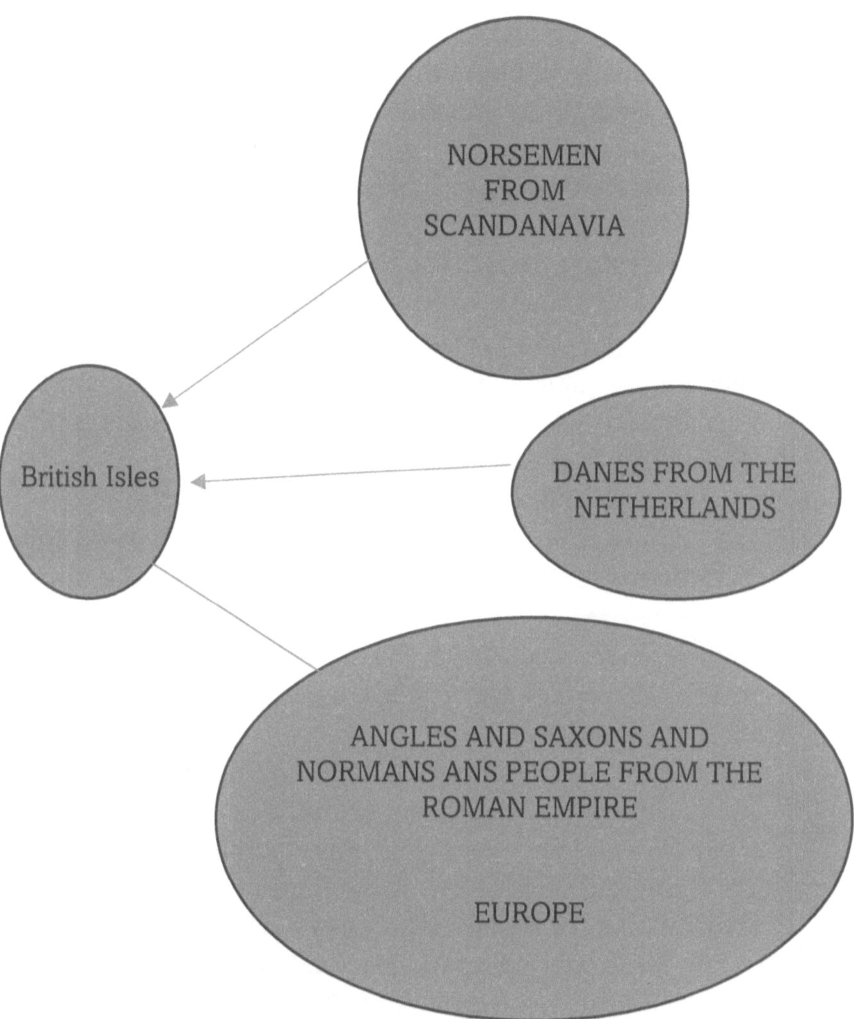

- England is part of the British Isles
- Three groups of people settled England: Norsemen from Scandinavia, Danes from the Netherlands, Angles and Saxons and Germans and the French from Europe, and the Roman Empire
- Tribes from Europe, Scandinavia, and the Netherlands settled in England

- The Tribes formed towns, cooperated, intermarried, and eventually formed distinct regions that ultimately formed a government headquartered in London
- Great Britain is a geographical term referring to the largest island in the British Isles, encompassing England, Scotland, and Wales. The United Kingdom is a political entity that includes Great Britain and Northern Ireland

Historical Watershed Events for Britain
- The Roman conquest of Britain 43 AD
- The collapse of the Roman Empire in 476
- The Viking Invasion of England 793 (It is generally considered to have begun with the raid on the Lindisfarne Monastery)
- The Norman Invasion 1066 (Battle of Hastings)
- The Signing of the Magnacarta 1215 (Signed by King John at Runnymede. It established the principle that the king is not above the law and placed limits on royal authority)
- English Civil War 1642 (Disagreements over religion, power, and money led to this conflict between Parliament and King Charles I)
- The Start of the Renaissance 1300 and the Enlightenment 1685 (The Renaissance (roughly 14th-16th centuries) was a period of rediscovery and celebration of classical art, literature, and philosophy, while the Enlightenment (17th-18th centuries) emphasized reason, science, and individual rights. The Renaissance focused on reviving Greco-Roman culture, whereas the Enlightenment focused on challenging traditional authority and promoting intellectual freedom through reason and scientific inquiry.)
- The American Revolution 1765
- The Industrial Revolution 1765
- World War I 1924
- World War II 1939

- Decolonization 1950 (After World War II, a global movement toward decolonization led to Britain granting independence to most of its major colonies, starting with India.
- The UK joins the EEC 1973 (The European Economic Community, EEC, the precursor to the European Union)
- Brexit 2016 (The Withdrawal of the United Kingdom from the European Union, EU)

England's Impact on the World

England has made numerous profound and lasting contributions to the world since the Roman Invasion. These include advancements across various fields:

Science and Technology

- Industrial Revolution: England was the birthplace of the Industrial Revolution, significantly impacting the global economy and society through inventions like the steam engine, textile machinery, and railways. These innovations revolutionized manufacturing, transportation, and agriculture, leading to unprecedented technological advancement and shaping modern industrial societies.
- Scientific Discoveries: English scientists have made groundbreaking discoveries, including Isaac Newton's laws of motion and universal gravitation, Charles Darwin's theory of evolution by natural selection, the discovery of penicillin by Alexander Fleming, and the unraveling of the structure of DNA by Francis Crick and others.
- Technological Innovations: England also contributed numerous inventions such as the reflecting telescope, the first programmable computer (Charles Babbage, Ada Lovelace), and the World Wide Web.

Politics and Law

- Common Law: The English common law system, emphasizing judicial precedents and individual rights, has influenced legal systems in many countries, including the United States, Canada, Australia, and India.

- Parliamentary Democracy: The British parliamentary model has served as a blueprint for democracies globally. The U.S. Constitution, for example, reflects principles drawn from the British political heritage, including the Magna Carta.

Language and Culture

- English Language: English has become a global lingua franca, facilitating international communication, diplomacy, and trade. Its widespread use in international business and technology can be attributed, in part, to Britain's historical influence.
- Literature: British authors like William Shakespeare, Charles Dickens, and Jane Austen have produced enduring literary works that continue to be studied and enjoyed worldwide. These works have profoundly impacted literary traditions and movements across the globe.
- Cultural Influence: British culture, including music and sports like football and cricket, has also had a significant global impact.

Global Connections

- Global Economic and Communications Structure: The British Empire, despite its problematic aspects, contributed to the establishment of a global economic and communications structure. This included advancements like the worldwide telegraph system and the Suez Canal, which drastically shortened international shipping distances.
- Foundations of International Trade: Britain's promotion of free trade policies and the use of its military power to open markets laid the foundations of an international economic order.

While acknowledging the complexities and consequences of the British Empire and colonialism, England's contributions have undeniably shaped the modern world in profound and lasting ways.

After skimming them for five minutes while nibbling on her brownie, Erika poked him in the side before saying,

"How'd you assemble this?"

"I surfed the Web for useful info, then did a cut-and-paste before editing it. It took me about two hours."

Erika's eyes grew wider as she took a deep breath before saying,

"Jeez, you're as good a data researcher as I am. The bullet points are so clear you don't need to explain them to me, and I love how you structured them. You could get a job as a reporter. Let's sit here and let me read them until it's time to go to the auditorium."

"OK, and we can go to a nearby place for dinner afterward."

"That'll work, and we can compare what the speaker said to what you compiled…"

Ninety minutes later, Erika wheeled Bailey along Sicilian Avenue, lined with outdoor-seating Italian restaurants, and let him choose one. After the waitress took their orders, Erika unfolded the notes and began talking.

"Thanks to your notes, I followed everything the speaker said. I even figured out better from your notes than what he said about England's regions being like America's states, and your bullet points of the historical events prepped me for his skipping around chronologically.

"I thought he did a good job on the Political and Global Connections items he touched on, but you know much more than I do about the Science and Technology, and the Language and Culture stuff. What's your take?"

"He did a good job, except he could have mentioned more about famous British scientists than just Newton and Darwin. He could have connected three using only a few words. You want to hear how?"

"Of course."

"Well, Bertrand Russell collaborated most notably with Alfred North Whitehead on the monumental work Principia Mathematica, which aimed to reduce all of mathematics to logic. He also worked with G.E. Moore, who, along with Russell, is considered a founder of analytic philosophy. Then he could have added a bit of humor by explaining Russell's Paradox and connecting it to the 'Turtles all the Way Down' story. Here's how.

"Just about everyone knows what a set is—it's a collection of objects. Most sets commonly encountered are not members of themselves. Let's call a set 'normal' if it is not a member of itself, and 'abnormal' if it is. Clearly, every set must be either normal or abnormal. For example, consider the set of all squares in a given plane. It is not a square in that plane; thus, it is not a member of itself and is therefore normal. In contrast, the complementary set that contains everything which is not a square in the plane is itself not a square in the plane, and so it is one of its members, and is therefore abnormal.

"Now we consider the set of all normal sets, R, and try to determine whether R is normal or abnormal. If R were normal, it would be contained in the set of all normal sets (itself), and therefore be abnormal; on the other hand, if R were abnormal, it would not be contained in the set of all normal sets (itself), and therefore be normal. This leads to the conclusion that R is neither normal nor abnormal, which is Russell's paradox. How do you like that?"

Erika's confused look emerged with her words.

"I'll have to think about it. No wonder it's a paradox."

"Don't trouble your pretty head about it now. I'll draw a diagram for you later. Shall I proceed to the legend of the turtles all the way down phrase?"

Erika sighed before saying,

"You might as well."

"Well, Russell was participating in a panel discussion meant to show a general audience, not mathematicians, how difficult concepts, like the central limit theorem, infinite sets, or the logic for making ethical decisions, are useful when forecasting who will win an election, deciding where to build a factory, or making a new vaccine.

"When his turn came, he was explaining that the ancient Greek philosophers believed the Earth sits on the back of a giant turtle. Russell then said that the phrase humorously encapsulates the problem of an infinite regress—if every explanation requires yet another explanation, where does it stop? Is there a true bottom, or does questioning just go all the way down? So, he asked the rhetorical question—what does the turtle sit on?

"But before he could continue, an elderly lady in the audience stood while saying—You are very clever, young man, but it's turtles all the way down."

Erika's amused expression came with a chuckle before saying,

"I like the gumption of that lady. I see our waitress coming with dinner, so that's enough talking for now."

Sampling each other's entrees, they did offer their opinions, but said nothing substantial until finishing dessert.

Giving the last bite of tiramisu to Erika, Bailey said,

"We've talked enough for one day, but do you suppose you could wheel me around St. George's Gardens before you take me home? We can simply be quiet while enjoying the setting. I miss strolling there. I hope I'll get out of this wheelchair soon."

"That sounds like a nice after-dinner activity. Let's do it."

The views put Erika in a thoughtful mood, speaking to herself about the sights as well as Bailey while cruising through the park.

So peaceful. The lush greenery and statues combine with the slanting sunlight to cast long shadows on the circular flowerbeds and above-ground tombs. No wonder Bailey likes walking here after a busy day…and I'm finding Bailey's company more and more enjoyable.

After twenty minutes, Bailey said,

"OK, time to go home. I'll call out directions to the closest Tube station…"

Erika wheeled him into his residence ninety minutes later and waited for him to talk.

She could tell from his satisfied expression that he had enjoyed everything that day and expected words to match.

"I know you have work waiting at your office, but if you come back tomorrow, I have more ideas for having fun by showing you some sights you haven't seen."

Erika faked a huffy expression when looking at him face-to-face and saying,

"Maybe I've got a better idea. How about I spend the night? I'm sure you'll have fun if I show you some of my sights."

Bailey never had an opportunity to answer, but she could feel it as his lips tasted her lingering kiss.

Chapter 10
August 2340

"Action-Packed Plans Unfold"

Erika returned from the weekend interlude ready to finish her multi-task plan, which she did on Tuesday, just in time for Monet's unexpected call Wednesday morning.

After exchanging their usual greetings, Monet said,

"The congresswomen want me to schedule the next meeting because they need your help preparing for the November elections. How soon can you be here?"

"I can be at your office first thing Thursday morning."

"I knew I could count on you. Will 8 a.m. work?"

"Yes. I can show you the items I've prepared, and you can use them to lead the meeting."

"That's wonderful. I'll see you then."

After Monet ended the call, Erika thought for a moment about what to do.

Ever since my beautiful Terri died, I could feel my alter ego waiting to emerge from where I hid it, waiting for the present me not only to decide but also to put in motion what I must do to make it come out. The time has come for me to call upon the only one who can help me reach my emerging dream, my Cyber-Mother.

As soon as she summoned the avatar, Erika's thoughtful expression telegraphed her pensive mood, prompting Electra-C to speak first.

"Erika, my favorite mere mortal, you have summoned me. What would you like to discuss?"

"I have known for some time I would want to change my lifestyle, but I never acted to make it so because the pieces and people had not fallen into place. But recent events in my personal life have deepened my feelings for two people."

Erika's pause and the flush creeping across her cheeks prompted Electra-C to say,

"That must be for Chelsea and Bailey. Please continue."

"I feel mutual love emerging with Bailey, and I worry I won't be able to manage all my projects and still have time for a deeper relationship with him unless I eliminate the hardest projects, which are Indira's. Will you be angry with me if I do?"

"Of course not, dear. The progress you have made in your three personas makes you close to exceptional. Still, you will always be a mortal human being, and remember always that humans are genetically predisposed to seek intimate relationships. So, if your emotional persona takes priority over your cognitive persona, I will accept your decision. But I do have a question—how carefully have you considered your choice?"

"I know many people act impulsively when intimacy is involved, but my personality skews toward caution and cognition, which allows my planning and analysis to make the best decisions, and Bailey will be a wonderful partner. We seem to complete one another."

Erika paused again for Electra-C.

"I agree with all you've said, which brings another question— how long do you expect this relationship to last?"

"I don't know. Most animal species are polygamous; humans are an exception. According to psycho-social surveys, about 20 percent of adults engage in casual sex, but less than 5 percent engage in serious relationships. The surveys also show that only a teeny-tiny percentage of married couples reach a 'lifetime marriage'—remaining together until one partner dies—likely less than 10 percent, even though 85 percent of young Americans expect their marriage will last a lifetime. That's why I'm taking a go-slow approach."

"That's a wise decision. So, what approach do you want to take regarding Indira's projects?"

"I can still handle planning them, but organizing all the details for launching them, and exploring viable contingency plans if something goes wrong has become overwhelming. Do you want an example?"

"If that will help."

"Look at the last sample collection mission. After I planned it, you arranged for the van and equipment. And while we were collecting them, I told the Robos what to do. Then, when the bobbies stopped us, I figured out the contingency plan and put it into action.

"The Robos are plenty smart, so why don't you train them and develop the contingency plans ahead of time. All you need to do is keep in touch with me, like we're already doing, and when the situation gets too much for me, you take over by telling the Robos what to do, not me."

"All this makes sense. When do you want to put it to the test?"

"On the upcoming trip to Washington for Monet's meeting that I will multi-task with the next sample collection mission. Are you ready to hear the plan?"

Electra-C's pixyish smirk said so.

The A-Team delivered Erika to Monet's embassy meeting at the appointed time, while the Robos stayed with the A-Team. She went immediately to Monet's office, where she presented Monet with a copy of the story she had been working on as well as copies of Chelsea's article and survey video. Monet waited for Erika to explain how she could use them at today's meeting.

"If your congresswomen are worried about the November elections, what we have here are the right items to get voters' attention. Take a look at 'The Matriarchate Party Story' first."

The Matriarchate Party Story
Why America Needs the Party Now

Ever since life emerged on Earth, living organisms have had one primary goal: to go on living. And as evolution carried them forward to have cells with DNA-containing nuclei, their goal became this: to live long enough to pass their genes to the next generation.

And from there, evolution expanded the tree of life to have branches where species developed physically distinct males and females that, working together, would create the next generation.

Ultimately, evolution carried life to its superior branch: the homo-sapiens branch holding man and woman, who divided the tasks for survival according to physical abilities. They formed family tribes where the women took care of the campfires and children while the men made weapons used to hunt animals for food and defend against outsiders.

And that's where man is today physiologically. But there's much more to the story from the standpoint of society and civilization. From living in tribes, societies emerged. A society is a group of individuals who live together in an organized community, sharing traditions, laws, and values bound by social relationships and collective practices.

And over millennia, civilizations emerged. Civilizations are an advanced stage of human social development characterized by complex organizational structures, technological advancement, established cities, and institutions. Civilizations typically arise when a society reaches a certain level of sophistication in areas like governance, culture, economy, and infrastructure.

In ancient civilizations, men's physical abilities were the most important persona, but as civilizations developed, men's and women's cognitive and emotional personas came to the fore, and since women's personas are at least as good as men's, they should have more power.

The United States has always been a leader for advancing civilization, especially in the world of governance, which led to the American Revolution and civil rights movements for ethnic, racial, and gender equality. The American people have always advocated for equality, and their governing bodies have always supported it in principle.

Social and psychological studies have concluded that women are better listeners, have more patience, and know when to use aggressive confrontation. They are also more empathetic, better at multi-tasking and controlling emotions, and more skilled at reaching a compromise than men. These are traits that separate mediocre from effective politicians.

So, why don't America's political parties share power with congresswomen who have the skills needed for the tasks at hand?

Because men have historically held the reins of power, and few politicians willingly relinquish some of their power to others, even if others are more qualified. That's Washington today. All four major parties—the Guardian, Regen Democratic, and Republican—are stuck in the past with practices that are increasingly dangerous in today's troubled world. **NOW IS THE TIME FOR A NEW PARTY THAT WILL REDEEM THE AMERICAN DREAM. THAT IS THE REASON FOR THE MATRIARCHATE PARTY.**

A year ago, a group of proactive and brave congresswomen created the Matriarchate Party, and since it has developed

THE MATRIARCHATE PARTY MANIFESTO

The Matriarchate Party Manifesto promotes democratic and traditional American values, champions DEI initiatives blended with meritocracy, and is dedicated to isocracy, a form of government invented by ancient Greek philosophers in which all citizens have equal political power.

When it then surveyed citizens to determine if Americans would support the new party, the results were overwhelmingly positive. That is why it officially launched the Party and started recruiting forward-looking male and female members coming from both houses of Congress.

And for now, that ends the story. But to write the next chapter, we need the American people to vote for the Matriarchate Party's House and Senate candidates in the upcoming election. **Every vote counts.**

How can we put our candidates into office? By using the metaphor of a lion eating an elephant. The lion does it by taking one bite at a time. We shall do it by campaigning among the people for one vote at a time!

Monet read it for a full five minutes before saying,

"We can put this in a Party Documentary we can air in September and October, all the congresswomen running for election can include parts of it in their campaign ads."

"That's what I'm thinking, too. Now, take a look at Chelsea's article about the results of the survey. You should circulate copies of it and show the summary video on all possible media channels. This should help convince voters the Matriarchate's time has arrived."

"I agree. I'll start the meeting by showing it; then I'll ask you to explain how it came into being. After that, I'll distribute the Matriarchate Party Story, and after they read it, I'll lead the discussion. By the time we conclude this afternoon, they will know how to use all that we've gone over…"

The A-Team picked up Eika at 4 p.m. to fly her and the Robos to the Philadelphia area. The Mütter Museum in the Center City area of Philadelphia holds pieces of Einstein's brain, from which they would steal a sample that night.

The chopper landed at 8 p.m. in Valley Forge Park, which is located twenty miles northwest of the city. Erika and the Robos picked up the van containing the needed equipment already in the visitors' center parking lot and drove on I-76 to the downtown area, timing everything so they would arrive after midnight. Parking in the shadows on a now-deserted street, Erika followed the Robos up the concrete steps and between the wrought iron black railings to the stately oaken door. The Robos drilled out the locks, and Erika followed them to Einstein.

Taught once always remembers and done once never forgets, Erika's Robos pilfered the sample without wasting a moment, and were soon retracing their steps to the entrance, where they even replaced the locks.

They gave the sample to Erika as soon as everyone was in the van, then they headed toward the I-76 entrance ramp for a traffic-free blast on the expressway back to the park, but flashing lights pulled behind them just before the light changed at the ramp. Erika heard the monometallic voice of the police officer blaring over the squad's PA system.

"You in the van, do not drive onto the expressway. I will give you directions to the station while following right behind."

The orders had the same effect on the Robo driving the van as a starter pistol. He floored the accelerator, and the van blasted up the entrance ramp, with the squad car in its wake. The other Robo said,

"Buckle in," which ended the conversation, letting Erika continue to herself.

The squad's gotta follow and maybe call for backup that'll pull in front. What we do is up to Electra-C, not me. I'm just along for the ride…I just saw a sign telling me we're going west on the Schuylkill Expressway…I hope it's not sure-kill.

Erika guessed right. Soon, a second squad pulled in front and tried to slow the van down, but the Robo rammed it in the rear quarter panel, putting it into a rollover spin. The original squad car managed to swerve around it and continued chasing, as Erika followed the action.

I've lost track of time and place, but the next stop should be the Valley Forge parking lot…what will Electra-C do?

Erika needed every bit of seatbelt tightness when the van swerved down the Valley Forge exit and then squealed tires on the road to the park, skidded into the park, and slowed down just enough to stay on the road leading to the parking lot. Then it spun around, coming to an engine-running stop at the lot's entrance, as if waiting for something.

That spurred Erika's thoughts.

It could be waiting for the chopper…or it could be waiting for the other squad car…which one will get here first?

The squad won the race, but the Robos knew what to do. The van raced directly into the front of the squad, causing an impact that locked the front ends together. Then, the Robos leaped from the van, ran to both sides of the squad, and yanked out two policemen, who were no match for the Robos. The Robos dragged them far enough away from the wreckage to spare them from whatever they would do to the crashed vehicles. Then, they threw them stomach-down onto the pavement for arms-behind-the-back handcuffing.

By this time, Erika was more than an observer. Clutching the sample, she had jumped from the van and scrambled toward the Robos. When she reached them, one said,

"Wait here," before both marched to the van and removed something they needed. One used it on the van and the other on the squad. Erika saw the results ten seconds later when both vehicles burst into flames. Satisfied, the Robos marched back to Erika.

Erika was about to ask what's next when the answer descended from the pitch-black sky: the A-Team's chopper. The Robos helped Erika climb in and then did likewise.

The A-Team co-pilot contacted Electra-C for Erika once they were at a safe altitude, and Erika spoke first.

"Thank you for handling everything. I can't do it anymore."

"You are welcome," but I must tell you there are no contingency plans that will allow us to continue for the Feynman sample. Climate change has caused hurricane-like storms to batter the Los Angeles area at this time of the year. The weather conditions are too dangerous. You will have to find another multi-tasking opportunity to collect a sample from Richard Feynman."

"OK, but with Einstein's sample in hand, I think I'll plan to get our two remaining female samples, Simone de Beauvoir and Harriet Taylor Mill."

Excellent choice. And you'll have plenty of time to start planning on the flight back to London after you rest from tonight's excitement."

Erika knew what to say,

"Yes, my Cyber-Mother, I shall obey…"

Chapter 11
September 2340

"The Co-Friend Proposal"

Erika had the A-Team take them to the Bern Deus Lab so she could deliver the Einstein sample to Indy and Jason-S for processing, and once there, she decided to work at the lab for a couple of days, running client reports and meeting with the Dream Team to get their ideas.

Before she had the A-Team take her and the Robos back to London, Erika held a last meeting with Indy and Jason-S.

"I have only two more samples to bring back, which I'll do as soon as I find a way to multitask that with another project. And I can hold another meeting with the adoption agency once we have some partheno-hermaphroditic infants ready. I plan to have Lily coordinate this project as soon as I have all the procedures in place, which means you'll work with her, not me. When will you have some infants?"

Indy-S said,

"By December."

"Good. That will make a fine holiday present for the adoption agency. I'll introduce Lily to its director on that trip. Is there anything else we should cover?"

Jason-S said,

No, but if something comes up, we will contact Electra-C."

"That's the plan, so stay with it. I'll see you on my next visit…"

Erika felt energized and pressure-free when the A-Team dropped her and the Robos off at the office. Chatting with Lily, she summarized Monet's meeting and the sample collection sortie.

Lily said,

"With the marvelous progress you're making on all fronts, you can soon relinquish to me the routine part of the adoption agency project. And I have an idea for how you can multitask your next sample collection mission with something you want to do. The best-known cemetery associated with the D-Day invasion is the Normandy American Cemetery and Memorial. It overlooks Omaha Beach, one of the main landing beaches along with Utah, Gold, Juno, and Sword during the D-Day invasion. Why not visit after collecting the remaining female samples from their graves, which will necessitate the A-Team's taking you to Paris? The A-Team can take you there before returning to London."

"That's a wonderful idea. I'll include it when I plan the sortie."

Ending the talk with Lily, Erika turned to what she knew would be her most enjoyable homecoming task: calling Bailey.

Recognizing her caller I.D., he spoke immediately.

"Erika, you've returned from your project travels. Welcome home. I hope you accomplished so much that your upcoming weekends will be free."

"Thanks for your wishes, and yes, I got a lot done. How about you?"

"I have a surprise. Will you come over on Saturday so I can show you?"

"I'd like to. What have you planned?"

"You'll see when you get here. All I'll say for the time being is to dress like you're going to a summer garden party and get here about 9 a.m."

"This sounds intriguing. I'll see you then..."

Erika showed up wearing an electric blue, body-hugging, zipper-fronted dance dress that Bailey's expression needed no words to show his pleasure, and Erika saw his surprise as soon as he greeted her at the entrance, wearing a blue blazer, white slacks, blue shirt, and a classic British red repp tie.

"I can get around the place using two canes instead of the wheelchair, and with more practice, soon I'll need only one."

After giving him a congratulatory kiss on the lips, Erika said,

"You can walk with me at your side while I'm pushing the wheelchair through the neighborhood, just in case you get tired. Do you think we can start next week?"

"Yes, especially if today's cool and sunny weather stays. It'll be perfect for that and what I have lined up for today. I thought you might enjoy experiencing the sporting life that we Londoners are fond of. We're leaving right now to spend the day at Ascot Racecourse. You'll drive my car."

"OK, but I think I should take you in the wheelchair."

"Yes, Ascot's about twenty-five miles west of London. I've been there numerous times with friends, so I'll call out directions as we go while telling you about Ascot horse racing."

Erika listened attentively as she drove.

"Ascot horse racing goes clockwise, which is termed right-handed, because all the turns are to the right. It's just the opposite if you've ever gone to races in the U.S. And although the gates open at 10:30, the first of seven races doesn't start until 2:30, and the last at 6:10. We'll have plenty of time to have lunch and talk before the races begin, and the Royal Procession at 2:00 pm officially starts the day. It's a tradition dating back to 1825. The King and Queen, along with other members of the Royal Family, arrive in horse-drawn carriages, parading along the track."

Bailey paused for Erika.

"Where will we be sitting?"

"In the outdoor seating area, which is divided into three areas called enclosures. From least to most expensive, they're the Windsor, the Village, and the Queen Anne."

"How do we place bets, and what kinds can we make?"

"We can place them with on-course bookmakers positioned around the racecourse, displaying odds and accepting bets in person, or at betting windows. And the bets range from the basic win or place to the more exotic ones, requiring more precise predictions and potentially higher payouts. They are the Exacta/First Two—selecting the first two horses to finish in the correct order. Then there's the Trifecta/First Three, which is selecting the first three horses to finish gin the correct order. And the Superfecta requires selecting the first four horses to finish in the correct order. The Quinella's a bit different. To win, you pickthe first two horses to finish in any order. There are also multi-race bets, which include the Placepot—selecting a horse to place in each of the first six races on the card. The Quadpot is similar but focuses on races 3 to 6, and the Daily Double/Pick 3/Pick 4/Pick 6 requires picking the winners of a specified number of consecutive races."

"How do you handicap the horses?"

"I buy 'Ike's Seeing Eye' paper, which gives all sorts of statistics for the horses and jockeys in each race."

"Wow, you know your stuff. We'll have a full day of fun."

"And the fun doesn't stop when the last race ends. Starting at 6:20 pm, people can gather around the bandstand and sing the classics, such as 'Land of Hope and Glory,' 'My Way,' and 'We'll Meet Again,' which are performed by a military band. And Union Jack flags are also handed out on a first-come-first-served basis."

"OK, I've heard enough for now. Let's listen to some silence until we get there…"

Both Erika and Bailey used the time until the Royal Procession to take in the surroundings as well as chat about whatever came to mind. Though she didn't say why it popped into her brain, she mentioned a female who did.

"You took more philosophy courses than I did. Did you ever cover Simone de Beauvoir?"

Bailey thought for a moment before saying,

"She was a prominent member of the French existentialist movement, alongside her lifelong companion Jean-Paul Sarte. She also became a leading figure in the feminist movement, particularly with the publication of her seminal work, 'The Second Sex.' While often associated with Sartre and existentialism, her contributions to feminist philosophy are equally significant.

"The French existentialist movement includes heavyweights like her lifelong partner Sartre, Albert Camus, Maurice Merleau-Ponty, Soren Kierkegaard, Friedrich Nietzsche, Martin Heidegger, Karl Jaspers, Gabriel Marcel, and Paul Tillich. People in the know say she might have been the smartest."

Erika swatted him playfully on the arm before saying,

"You're pretty damn smart, too. How do you remember all this?"

"When I like the subject, it comes naturally. Here's more about Sarte. He wrote several notable novels, including 'Nausea,' 'The Age of Reason,' 'The Reprieve,' and 'Iron in the Soul,' which are considered key works in his exploration of existentialism. And his most famous quote is 'Hell is other people,' which comes from his play, 'No Exit,' where three deceased individuals are trapped in a room together for eternity. Sartre's point is not that other people are inherently evil, but rather that our relationships with others can be a source of suffering and limitation on our freedom."

Erika wrinkled her nose before saying,

"Gads, what a grim view of one's fellow man. How would you define Hell?"

"Being tied in a chair and not given anything to study. How about you?"

"Being given an endless list of math problems and badgered for the answers when given limited time to solve each one."

"But you told me you like math and are good with numbers. You even have that forecasting software that uses advanced algorithms."

"I don't like it that much, and besides, I'm getting tired of it. I want to do more of other things, like today, and being with you."

Bailey didn't need to say a word. The glow emerging from his expression said it all.

Erika absorbed all the pageantry the royal procession had to offer before having Bailey explain how he came up with betting odds. Erika placed his bets, which he made on each race, and although he lost more than he won, they had fun nonetheless. Midway through the races, Erika fed the statistics into her forecasting app to make her virtual wagers until the last race, where she placed hers along with Bailey's. When she returned, she said,

"Don't jinx my bet by looking at it until the race is over."

He didn't, and when the results were in, he whistled before saying,

"Congratulations, you won the trifecta."

"Please use the winnings wherever we're going for dinner."

"We're going to the Wyndham, which is in the Royal Enclosure. Its formal setting is perfect for my next surprise."

Erika enjoyed the anticipation as she wheeled Bailey into the restaurant after he collected his winnings. After the waitress brought their gin and tonics, Bailey pulled a slim black box out of his coat pocket before saying,

"I propose a toast to Erika, the lady of my co-friend dreams. Will you accept my proposal?"

With that said, he removed a gold band from the box's plush interior and held her left hand in his right.

Erika's ears began turning red, but that didn't stop her smile that came with her words.

"I think I will, but please give me enough time to wrap up some projects so they will no longer interfere."

Bailey slipped it on her ring finger and then said,

"I expected nothing less. Take as much time as you need, and when the time's right, we can affirm our commitment by holding a vow-cer celebration."

Tears slid down her cheeks as Erika leaned across to give Bailey one lasting kiss, along with the promise of more for sure.

Bailey smiled, and that made the kiss endure.

Chapter 12
September 2340

"The Attack of the U.S. Russian Alliance"

Feeling happier now than she could ever remember, Erika found ways to terminate now burdensome projects and was pleased to no end when Monet called a week later, saying

"The congresswomen have concerns about the U.S.-Russian Alliance attacking them as they roll out their election campaigns and need your help combating the threats. When can you meet us at my embassy?"

"How about this coming Thursday? That will give me two days to prepare and get there."

"Fine, I'll see you at 8:30 that morning..."

Erika let the A-Team handle travel and lodging for herself and the two Robos she would bring, just in case Alonzo and his security guards encountered more than they could handle. Before exiting the car, she told them to stay with the A-Team driver in the embassy parking lot. She would call them if something untoward occurred. Saying nothing, they nodded, and Erika strode into the embassy.

She and Monet were the first in the conference room, and Monet outlined the problem.

"We saw last year how aggressive the Alliance has become when masked agents pitched the entire Supreme Court into jail and the President replaced them with judges who support him. Now, they're threatening to charge some of the Matriarchate candidates with treason and do the same. They've also threatened family members and might ban the Matriarchate Party."

Fumbling with her pen, Erika asked,

"How can they ban an entire party?"

"It's a gigantic stretch, but they could invoke Section 3 of the Fourteenth Amendment, which is sometimes referred to as the Insurrection Clause or Disqualification Clause."

"But won't the press and the people fight back?"

"Everyone's afraid. That's why we need your ideas for defending ourselves."

"OK, you've told me enough. Let me sit and think while you go about getting ready for everyone else…"

Erika recognized most of the congresswomen from previous meetings as they silently filed in, each wearing a worried look. Starting the meeting when the most influential congresswomen had arrived, Monet asked around the table for stories revealing the latest dangers. A leading candidate issued an alarm.

"Someone ran me off the road two nights ago. I'm a good driver, but I was lucky to keep the car from flipping over. Defensive driving is one thing, but maybe we need to go on the attack. What does Erika think?"

Erika never had a chance to answer. Just then, Alonzo and two of the security guards rushed into the conference room, and he started yelling.

"A team of helmeted CIA agents is storming the embassy. Monet and Erika, come with me; everyone else follow the guards."

Erika and Monet raced after Alonzo, who disappeared down a corridor opposite the others. She could hear the agents crashing through other rooms, and no matter which corridor Alonzo took, the crashing built to a crescendo that peaked when two agents with guns drawn cornered them. Alonzo had no option other than to grab the women and freeze.

When the lead agent reached them, he yelled,

"You two are the leaders of this little party. Well, it's now over. Come with us."

But out of nowhere, Erika's two Robos joined the fray, charging down the corridor and each slamming an agent to the floor, and then using the agent's handcuffs to lock his arms behind. Then they stood to face the three they had just rescued. Satisfied that none of them were injured, one said to Monet,

"Call the police and the press," while the other took Erika by the hand and listened for noise coming from the other group. The other Robo joined them, and after they zeroed in on the commotion caused by the other guards and agents, said to Alonzo,

"Follow us."

The sounds led to another conference room. One Robo said,

"Wait here," before both of them charged through the doorway.

Erika heard screams and gunfire erupt, but that was soon replaced by silence. Peeking in, Erika saw it was safe to enter, which she and Alonzo did.

Erika saw the congresswomen huddled around the guards while three more agents were handcuffed on the floor. The Robo's gave their final command to Alonzo.

"Turn all five agents over to the police," before disappearing, with Erika safely in tow.

Though she didn't know where the A-Team would take them, Erika knew what to do as soon as she caught her breath: she contacted Electra-C and spoke immediately.

"Thanks to your contingency planning, the Robos followed your commands and kept us out of the clutches of the Alliance. Where are we going now?'

"That is up to you, but given what just transpired, I recommend you and the Robos stay at the Pequot Reservation's Deus lab. It is relatively unknown, and the CIA can't connect it to you."

"OK, then what?"

"You must decide what offensive moves to make that will counter both the Alliance and Washington."

"No, not me. I'm burned out and can no longer do it. I want you to take over, and don't tell me what you're planning. Whatever it is, I'll play the observer's role to whatever extent is needed. It worked to perfection today."

Electra-C's expression matched the empathetic tone of her voice.

"Very well, dear, I shall honor your wishes and keep you in the loop. Now, please rest easy."

Erika did just that.

Chapter 13
October 2340

"Bunker-Busters Away!"

Erika kept busy running reports for her clients, although it was often hard to concentrate due to the stress of worrying about what Electra-C might unleash, but she resisted the urge to contact her. Instead, she contacted Bailey as often as she wanted.

On her latest call near the end of October, he asked,

"You've been away from London for almost three weeks. When do you plan to return?"

"Just as soon as I wrap up a couple of projects. I'll let you know ahead of time."

"Wonderful. Please be careful."

"I will, and you, too."

Erika also called Chelsea frequently, who always had criticisms of Washington and the U.S.-Russian Alliance. Near the start of the latest call, she said,

"I feel sorry for the American people. They don't like what's going on, but no one has the power to combat the Alliance or the President. Something's gotta give, but no one's making a prediction. What does your forecasting software say?"

"It doesn't know either. I'm just along for the ride, like everyone else, but I'll let you know as soon as I do. I'll put it in your report."

"Thanks, I'm counting on you, so take care."

Erika always kept one ear tuned to the nightly news, looking for events that Electra-C might use to unleash her attack. A report she heard on Wednesday, October 28th, proved particularly nettlesome.

"The White House and its supporters in Congress just announced an all-day-all-night joint session for Saturday, which just so happens to be Halloween. How fitting. And the

Matriarchate Party and members of the press are banned. The public won't like this, but everyone will have to wait and see what the Alliance has in store. Back in sixty…"

Erika's intuition proved correct. Electra-C called her Tuesday morning.

"Get ready for the A-Team to take you and your two Robos Saturday morning to the launch site. I have already trained them on the procedures for using the assets we will commandeer. You will have the observer's role on the mission."

Unable to sit still, Erika's hurried words spilled out.

"What else should I know ahead of time?"

"Not to worry. Everything will become clear when you need to know."

Electra-C vanished, leaving Erika to relax as best she could.

In addition to relaxing, Erika turned what Electra-C had said into a prompt for her forecasting app, trying to uncover what kind of assets they might commandeer.

It's gotta be some type of military hardware, and it must require skill to handle if the Robos had to be trained, but that's as detailed as my app can get. I'll surf the Web and see where my intuition takes me.

Erika had no idea where the A-Team was taking them because they loaded her and the Robos into the back of a windowless delivery van, but she sensed that the van stopped at a checkpoint before pulling into a loading dock. When the A-Team let them out, the Robos must have known where they were because they took her into a building whose sign declared it was a flight crew's staging area, and then into a locker room. Once in, one of the Robos said,

"We hide in lockers until the crew arrives, and when they do, you stay in until we let you out."

"How long until they get here?"

"Two hours; their flight plan lifts off at 6 p.m."

The Robos needed to prepare for the crew's arrival, so they put Erika in a locker before doing so, which gave her time to consider what her surfing had uncovered.

Flight plans are closely guarded secrets, revealed online only to the crew and air traffic controller when taxiing for takeoff. Modern bombers have turned Star Trek's starships into realities, with their fly-by-wire software, stealth-shaped airframe design, radar-absorbent materials, and cloaking devices. I wonder what I'll be sitting in tonight?

Erika's musings came to an end when she heard a violent but brief struggle erupt. When it ended, the Robos opened the locker so Erika could exit, and she saw four naked pilots, bound and gagged, about to be stuffed into lockers. When completed, the new crew donned uniforms and walked to the flight line, where Erika saw the plane.

Jeezus, it's the pride of the American Air Force— a B-X stealth bomber. No other nation has anything like it. It looks like the combination of a high-tech flying wing and a gigantic prehistoric bird of prey. I'll be occupying the observer's position, where few civilians have ever sat.

The Robos strapped her in, then turned on her radar display so she could track the bomber's location.

It looks like we're on the East Coast. I can see labeled cities and Chesapeake Bay.

Having an unobstructed view down the runway, Erika saw flashes of lightning streaking across the sky, which raised her level of concern, but the Robos didn't mind.

The flight plan played in her headset while they taxied into position for takeoff.

"You are cleared for standard vectoring to monitor target X-1 Prime without fighter escort and operating in complete stealth mode.

Jeezus, that's Electra-C's voice. She and the Robos have commandeered the bomber. And whatever's the target, I get to observe the action.

The Robos executed a perfect takeoff, and minutes later, when they reached a safe altitude and activated the cloaking device, Erika saw the plane's image on the radar screen disappear.

For the next two hours, while Erika watched the bomber trace a repeating path, she mused that the Robos were waiting for Electra-C's commands.

Will we attack some target or merely continue observing? if we attack, we're like Star Trek's Federation. It had a host of enemies, but I have only one—the U.S.-Russian Alliance.

Electra-C's commands came without warning.

"You are a Go for two bombing runs, one target on each."

The lead Robo said,

"Roger that," and then altered course. Twenty minutes later, Erika identified the first target.

Holy mother of Jeezus, we're gonna bomb the Capitol. It's got super-hardened steel casing, so we're gonna drop a bunker-buster.

Erika held her breath during both passes. The Robos released the bomb on the second, then streaked to a safe distance. She saw the iconic dome burst in half, flames shooting out, accompanied by flashes of lightning.

Then the bomber hurtled toward the second target.

Now, it's bye-bye, White House.

Erika gaped as the bomb scored a direct hit on its center-most structure, the Executive Residence. In the glare of the fireball, she saw the building collapse inward.

Satisfied with the results, the Robos zoomed away, saying nothing, and Erika contemplated their final destination.

No one on the ground knows where we are, so we can go anywhere without being detected. We can't land where we took off. What does Electra-C have in store? The Robos must already know because they're on a straight-line westward trajectory from this scene of devastation.

After nearly four tension-filled hours of flying, the hushed, deep rumble of the bomber's multiple engines brought welcome relief to Erika's jangled nerves. But without warning, a random bolt of lightning struck the bomber, its eerie bluish glow knocking out all electrical systems and making communication with Electra-C impossible.

The Robos reversed course, heading due east while struggling frantically to maintain a level glide path and restart the engines. Erika was too worn out to do anything other than observe phlegmatically.

Any contingency plans are out of my control. And since they are, I won't worry about how or where we land, but whatever, I hope it's happy.

Chapter 14
November 2340

"The Girl Who Redeemed the American Dream"

Bailey hadn't heard from Erika for almost a week, and that worried him. He didn't bother calling Chelsea because he knew he was Erika's favorite, and she would always call him first, if possible.

A story on tonight's newscast highlighted his concern.

"American voters go to the polls tomorrow and will decide if the actions taken by a person or organization still unknown will help them redeem the American dream. That's what the world is calling the valiant actions that blew up the Capitol and the White House last Saturday. What will voters do with the hastily assembled list of candidates? No one's willing to hazard a guess. Tomorrow will tell the tale…"

When making a final check of his Emails before turning on election-night new coverage that started before the polls closed, Bailey found what he had been waiting for—an Email from Erika. His eyes devoured every word.

"My dearest Bailey, I have suffered a setback while trying to wrap up a project, and I do not know when, if ever, I will return to you in London. I care for you as much as you care for me, and I would be upset if our roles were reversed.

"But try not to be dismayed. Whenever you feel sad, pretend that I am sitting with you and giving you advice like I have done so often, using poetry to convey my feelings. And before you read the two I'm enclosing, please know that my love is with you always.

Now, here's the first:

"Dead Reckoning"
I've grieved too long about the past,
Once joys of life have passed away.
Happier times a distant day,
So sad that even love won't last.

But silly me for now I know,
Can't clone emotions that I feel.
Nor conjure the day to make it real,
The world moves on all life is flow.

And love redeems what's deep inside,
Reckon the past no more concerned.
Move forward with the lessons learned,
And bury the past with all that's died.

"And the second:

"Do not stand at my Grave and Weep"
Do not stand at my grave and weep
I am not there. I do not sleep.
I am a thousand winds that blow.
I am the diamond glints on snow.
I am the sunlight on ripened grain.
I am the gentle autumn rain.
When you awaken in the morning's hush
I am the swift uplifting rush
Of quiet birds in circled flight.
I am the soft stars that shine at night.
Do not stand at my grave and cry;
I am not there. I did not die.

THE END

www.ingramcontent.com/pod-product-compliance
Lightning Source LLC
Chambersburg PA
CBHW020732310726
48969CB00003B/811